PENGUIN BOOKS

THE SUMMER OF LETTING GO

Catherine Dellosa plays video games for a living, reads comics for inspiration, and writes fiction because she's in love with words. She lives in Manila, Philippines, with her husband, whose ideas fuel the fire in her writing.

Her young adult fantasy novel *Of Myths and Men* has been published by Penguin Random House SEA and is her love letter to gamer geeks, mythological creatures, and epic quests to save the world. The second book in the trilogy, *Of Life and Lies*, is out now.

When it comes to contemporary YA, *For the Win: The Not-So-Epic Quest of a Non-Playable Character* is another tribute to gaming that's all about the heartbreak of unrequited love.

She has also penned *The Choices We Made (And Those We Didn't)*, published by BRUMultiverse, as well as *Raya and Grayson's Guide to Saving the World* and *The Bookshop Back Home* as part of #romanceclass—a community of Filipino authors who are equally in love with words.

When she's not lost in a land of make-believe, she works as a games journalist for one of the biggest mobile gaming media outlets in the UK. She one day hopes to soar the skies as a superhero, but, for now, she strongly believes in saving lives through her fiction. Check out her books at bit.ly/catherinedellosabooks or follow her on FB/IG/Twitter at @thenoobwife.

ADVANCE PRAISE FOR
THE SUMMER OF LETTING GO

'From the first page, this heartwarming story of love, loss, and family draws you in and won't let go.'

—Marga Ortigas, author of
The House on Calle Sombra and
There Are (No) Falling Stars in China

'Lyrical, thoughtful, with a tinge of bittersweetness, *The Summer of Letting Go* is a poignant look at first love, family, and heartbreak. Dellosa's prose tugs at your heartstrings, and her characters are always relatable, solidifying her as one of the rising stars in YA fiction.'

—Joyce Chua, author of *Until Morning*

'Catherine's *The Summer of Letting Go* is a must-read for those looking for a heartrending yet heartwarming tale that explores love and loss in a quietly breathtaking manner.'

—Leslie W, author of
The Night of Legends trilogy

'Gripping, poignant . . . just lovely! Catherine Dellosa is the queen of young love and teen romance.'

—Eva Wong Nava, author of
The House of Little Sisters

Also by Catherine Dellosa

The Summer of
Letting Go

Catherine Dellosa

PENGUIN BOOKS
An imprint of Penguin Random House

PENGUIN BOOKS

Penguin Books is an imprint of the Penguin Random House group of
companies whose addresses can be found at
global.penguinrandomhouse.com

Published by Penguin Random House SEA Pte Ltd
40 Penjuru Lane, #03-12, Block 2
Singapore 609216

First published in Penguin Books by Penguin Random House SEA 2024

10 9 8 7 6 5 4 3 2 1

The Summer of Letting Go includes elements that might not be suitable
for some readers. Death and grief are present in the story. Readers who
may be sensitive to these elements please take note.

ISBN 9789815127799

Typeset in Garamond by MAP Systems, Bengaluru, India

www.penguin.sg

To the ghosts that haunt us all, I hope you like Cheetos

Contents

Cheetos Are Mankind's Greatest Invention

Nowhere Else for Me to Be

Uncle Drew always said that fate is fixed, love is a thunderstorm, and Cheetos are mankind's greatest invention since medicine and stuff.

He gave me a pair of earrings shaped like Cheetos bags when I was eight—some random junk made of polymer clay and cheap hooks he found at a comic con bazaar. The hooks gave way a long time ago, but I kept the mini Cheetos bags— one I refashioned into a pendant and the other into a keychain for my bag. I don't share his undying love for Cheetos, but the gift was a different thing.

Plus, 'medicine and stuff' was exactly what he had said too, like he couldn't be bothered to get the technical details right. He would talk a lot like that back then, but he's always been super chill and all, and I guess I get that from him.

I don't think I've ever made too much of an effort in school, and I've never had much of a problem precisely because there's been nothing I've wanted badly enough to care.

Which is why when I saunter into the tea shop for the first time with my resume in one hand and a clenched fist in the other, the owner's answer takes me completely by surprise.

'You're hired.' He slides my so-called CV over the counter back to me. The completely blank space on the lower half of the semi-crumpled paper looks like it's mocking me. 'Aprons at the back.'

'You mean I . . . I got the job?' I stare at him with my mouth hanging open, and he shrugs. The manager-slash-owner of this little cafe-that-could looks like he's in his early twenties, his hair flopping over his forehead and a single stud earring in his left ear. Despite the casual look, he's giving off the complete opposite vibe—the kind that tells me he won't appreciate me slacking off on the clock.

He finishes tying his own apron around his waist and frowns at me. 'Yes. You're not going to keep making me repeat myself, are you?'

'Uh, no. I mean, no sir. I mean, yes—aprons at the back.' I fumble for my haphazard resume and stuff it into my backpack. 'I just . . . didn't think I'd start right away.'

The steely, almost dark grey eyes narrow at me. 'Do you see anyone else around here?'

I glance at the length of the counter. 'Um, no?'

'No. So,' he nods his head toward the door of the stockroom, 'aprons at the back.'

'Yes. Okay. Um, thank you, sir.' I scooch behind the counter beside him with my heart in my throat.

He shakes his head. 'Just Luca.'

'Right. Thanks, Luca.' I toss him a smile and he almost smiles back.

Almost.

The stockroom is a cramped space with one wall stacked high with random kitchen supplies and another with a shelf of tea leaves. Given that I have absolutely no experience working before this, much less making tea, I'm not too sure why I've got the job. I marched in here prepared to get shot down, but I really, really want this, and maybe I just happened to saunter in at the exact time and moment that Luca needed some help, or maybe he was in a good mood, or maybe Uncle Drew's 'fate is fixed' thing is actually totally true.

I slide my backpack off my shoulder onto the small table in the corner of the stockroom. I'm not about to question the hands of fate and all that, because this is exactly where I want to be.

And maybe one day, when the sadness is gone and all that's left is nothing, maybe this'll be my home too, because then there'll be nowhere else to go.

I swipe one of the nametags on the table and scribble K-A-L-I underneath the words that say, 'Hi! I'm _____'. Then, I stick the label onto my chest, hoping to mark myself forever. As I pluck one of the beige aprons hanging by a rack and tie it around my waist, I let out a long, drawn-out breath.

I'm here, Uncle Drew. I smile to myself. *I can finally see you every day.*

* * *

Five hours later, the last customer of the day, some self-important woman who didn't hang up her phone the whole time she was here, heads out. Luca leaves me behind the counter and follows her, locking the front door after her.

It's a cosy little nook, Tea for Two. There are only four tables that fill a tiny corner of the ground floor in this two-storey building, an old-ish structure that's a revolving door of shops, cafes, and hangouts ranging from pop-up stores to late-night dim sum canteens. In all my student years, this very building's iteration has changed more times than Freyja's hair colour, but in Version Who-Knows-How-Many-Now, it's Tea for Two. There's a corner booth that's always hidden from the counter, and after spending my very first day as part of the workforce—or rather, the internforce—I can honestly say it's not that bad.

Besides, shadowing Luca behind the counter has its benefits. If I didn't have a hidden agenda behind applying to this job in the first place, I'd say he's pretty cute.

But I'm here for a reason, and not even a college dude who somehow looks elegant in a white shirt and plain jeans is going to distract me.

He turns back at me and raises his eyebrow. 'Well?'

Luca's less-than-pleasing personality is definitely helping with my no-distractions rule. 'Um. Yes?'

His grey eyes scan the menu up in chalk behind me then land back on mine. 'How was the first day?'

'Okay.' I watch as he strides up to me and leans his elbows on the counter between us. 'It's . . . not as overwhelming as I thought it would be.'

'Hmm.' He makes a low guttural sound as he's staring at me. Even when he's leaning against the counter like this, he's a head taller than I am. 'What time does your last class end?'

'I've a month off before graduation. I don't have classes this summer.'

'I can only afford to hire you for half a shift. Can I expect you to be here every day?'

'Yes. Of course.' It's only two streets away from school anyway and coming here is infinitely better than going home. 'That's why I applied for the job, didn't I?'

'Hmm.' He scrutinizes me again, the small space between me and the counter the only thing keeping us apart.

If I thought there would be a possibility of something happening between us, I would have blushed—but five hours with Luca and I can already tell it's the last thing on his mind.

'Good,' he finally grunts, launching himself away from the counter. He reaches behind him to untie his apron, folds it neatly in a proper square, and rests it on the countertop. 'Tomorrow at four then. Don't be late.'

'Oh.' I eye his apron on the counter and marvel at how he's somehow made each side completely equal to the other. 'I'm not locking up?'

He marches into the back room and I follow suit. 'I have to get back to my review.'

'Okay.' I try to swallow my disappointment. I'd rather not head home right now, but I guess there's nowhere else to go. 'Um, so I guess I'll see you tomorrow.'

Luca doesn't respond. In the silence of the empty tea shop, I bite back a sigh and start trudging to the counter.

'Hey, Kali?'

I whip back around. 'Yes?'

'You forgot your backpack.'

'Oh.' My heart sinks. I scoop up my things from the stockroom where Luca has now set up his little study nook on the table, three heavy textbooks sprawled out in front of him along with a laptop. There's a sticker that says, 'What would Batman do?' behind his screen that momentarily brings a smile to my lips.

I've barely taken another step out of the back room when he clears his throat.

'Yeah?'

This time, he doesn't even bother to look up from his notes. 'Your apron.'

'Right.' I untie it and fold it the same way he did but when I place the apron next to his, it just looks like I didn't even try at all.

I make an awkward beeline out from behind the counter, and the moment I'm alone in the tea shop, I settle down on the corner booth shielded from Luca's vision.

I peer at my smartwatch. 9.15 p.m.

'Hey, kiddo.'

Right on time.

I look up to see my uncle's smiling face, seated across from me in this tiny booth, his eyes filled with joy and mischief like he's got a million secrets he's just dying to tell me.

'Hey, Uncle Drew.' The brown and tattered newsboy cap is still on his head like it always used to be, and he's tilting his head at me with a hand in his pocket, just as chill as he was the last time I saw him. 'Did you wait long?'

'Nah. What's a few minutes to me nowadays, you know?' He shrugs. 'So, you're working here now?'

'Yeah. I wanted to make sure we could talk every day.' I smile at him. 'Is that okay?'

'Of course it's okay, but I'm not sure your mother would agree.' He smiles back like he just doesn't know what to do with me. 'Your mother does know, doesn't she?'

'Why? So she can stop me from doing this too?' I drop my backpack on the floor and lean back against my chair. 'No way. I'm not letting her in on this if it's the last thing I do.'

Uncle Drew sighs, folding his hands on the table. 'Well, I guess I'm not surprised you've got that rebellious streak in you. When I was your age, I was much, much worse.'

'I know. Your own mother wouldn't let me hear the end of it.' I grin. 'So, how long can you stay here and chat with me tonight?'

At this, Uncle Drew looks at me with a sad smile, the glorious moonlight streaming through the window behind him casting nothing against his body.

'I'm dead, Kali. There's nowhere else for me to be, is there?'

Always There, Always There

Fire_Drewid

World Boss at Laurel Field. Where are you

KaliShandy88

Dino Castle. 5 out of 8 tasks

Fire_Drewid

Forget the tasks. WORLD BOSS HERE NOW

KaliShandy88

I've been at this for an hour now, Uncle Drew! 3 tasks to go okay

Fire_Drewid

Your guild needs you, young one. More importantly, your druid needs you. Be my tank, Kali! I'm a sitting duck out here

KaliShandy88

Fiiiine I'm coming

Fire_Drewid

Don't let me die, kiddo

KaliShandy88

NEVER

'Refresh my memory.' Freyja shakes her long, natural waves, jolting me out of rereading Uncle Drew's old messages on my phone. 'How long do you plan on pretending you still have school?'

I shrug and put my phone down. 'As long as it takes.'

'And the fact that there are only five weeks to go before graduation means nothing to you?'

'Nothing whatsoever.' A little girl squeals in the pool in front of us, and I shift my position on the stone bench along the side of the common area. 'All the folks need to know is that school ends at four, and that I've got this little part-time job until nine before I can come home. Good deal, right?'

She shakes her head again, fiddling with the choker on her neck. 'I don't know, Kal. You're really pushing it.'

'Since when were they ever concerned about where I traipse off?' I plant my hands on the bench and lean back. 'You're one to talk, though. *Please* tell me your parents know about Ateneo.'

'They don't, and maybe they shouldn't.' Freyja tucks both her legs underneath her on the bench beside me. She studies the calluses on her fingers, the proud battle scars of her music, and sighs. 'We can't afford it.'

'You should at least try to ask. Or you might get in on a scholarship.'

'I didn't make it into the programme. All I have is regular admission, which means I can kiss being with Ryan goodbye.' Freyja flinches at her own mention of her boyfriend, just as the little girl swimming in the pool starts crying. The mother picks her up and drags her out of the water, the tiny five-year-old kicking and screaming.

Not many residents use the common pool area here in Freyja's condo compound despite the high heat of summer, and I guess I understand. With both towers peering down at you in the middle of this central ground floor for everyone to see, I wouldn't want to wade into the water in my swimsuit, either.

'Ryan's set on law school, huh?'

She nods, bites her lip, then turns away from the screaming kid and back to me. 'I don't blame him—his ambition is one of the reasons I like him so much. But if I can't join him on campus, music somehow doesn't seem like such a magical alternative.'

'Frey. You can't tell me your music's lost its appeal? I mean, I understand *Ryan's* dream—but what about yours?'

'I don't want to talk about it right now.' She sighs. 'Tell me about this job.'

I shrug. 'It's cool. Nothing too hectic. I get to see Uncle Drew every day, so . . .'

I'm staring at a wayward fly buzzing around near my right leg, but I can somehow feel my best friend's eyes boring a hole into my face. She always says this veil of grief has been wrapped around me since that fateful day, and I guess I've never really learned to shake it off.

It's comfortable under this veil. It helps me wear my sadness like it's a part of me now, and maybe it always will be.

'Kali.' She places her hand over mine, and I look up. I expect her to start chastising me again, but she smiles. 'That's . . . great. Really great.'

'Thank you,' I smile back, and we spend the next few minutes just staring at the rippling water on the pool as it struggles to reclaim its lost stillness after the little girl and her mother left. The chirping of a few birds punctuates the silence, the heavy summer air descending on us like we've just been left behind.

* * *

Class ends at four. I hit Send and eyeballed the three dots flashing back and forth on my phone, eager for Uncle Drew to say yes like he always did. It didn't take long before I got his reply (Sure thing, kiddo), and I shoved my phone back into my backpack.

The invisible grip tugging at my heart had been with me since I left the house this morning, and it hadn't loosened its hold all day. Arguing with my parents was a staple in our house, but that morning, they must've had a fresh wave of jerkiness wash over them and felt like they were in the mood to ruin my life.

A pre-graduation party. That was it. Everyone in class was going and, with my reputation as head cheerleader, I had to go—I was destined to go. But I was convinced that ruining my senior year was Number One on my parents' agenda, and they hadn't let up since the year started.

I hated them. I hated this life.

Thank God for Uncle Drew then, the only one who ever understood me. Sometimes, I wished he were my actual, real parent—he practically raised me anyway, so why not?

Which was why when the thought of coming home after school to a house of hate loomed closer and closer as the final bell rang, I just had to ask him to pick me up. He was busy with work or something, but he had never refused whenever I asked him for anything.

I couldn't go home. I wouldn't.

The bell finally rang to let us all off the hook, and dismissal waved its magic across the whole school. Students who were bored out of their minds just a second ago buzzed to life, grabbing backpacks and high-fiving and already spilling out into the hallway like too much jam on a sandwich. I spotted Freyja and Ryan lingering by their lockers off to one side of the hall, but I wasn't in the mood to mingle like I always did after class. My parents sucked, and Uncle Drew was supposed to pick me up, and I'd ask him to take me to the mall and maybe hang around forever until my Mom berated him into taking me home.

It had always been a thing, and Uncle Drew was my safety net when days were hard and the parentals were harder.

I burst through the double gates of the school grounds with my head down, and people knew me well enough not to bother me on days like this. I'd like to think it wasn't so much that they were afraid of me but that they respected my space—you don't get to be Queen Bee without a few unspoken perks.

It was a short walk to the corner cafe—not quite Tea for Two yet but something else. It was just two small streets away, and Uncle Drew might be a ton of things, but he was never late—not when it came to me. I'd strut to our usual meeting place and he'd already be standing there, always just standing there, the newsboy cap on his head and his hands in his pockets with a goofy smile on his face. He might have a bag of Cheetos, or he might not, but he was always there, always there.

That day, though, that day was different. Something about the lingering uncertainty in the air made everything feel like there was a ripple in time, and it felt like I was trudging to the corner cafe in slow motion, taking forever to get to where I wanted to be. There was an unsettling of sorts tingling in the atmosphere, like something was about to happen or something had already happened and maybe I was too clouded by my anger and stubbornness and teenage drama to sense it as it tried to push me away and spare me.

I wasn't spared, though—neither of us were.

Because the second I rounded the corner, the cafe in plain sight just a narrow street ahead of me, there was a commotion right in the middle of the road, and somehow, I already knew something was very, very wrong.

My mind struggled to grasp bits and pieces of the scene in front of me, trying its best to make sense of everything, to morph things back into focus. My body refused to move altogether, but my heart—my raging, aching, and fearful heart—went feral. It was clawing against my chest, threatening to burst out of my ribs to escape this simple madness, this seemingly ordinary thing that ordinarily happened on what was supposed to be an ordinary day.

From where I was standing, I could still see him—Uncle Drew with his newsboy cap at the corner cafe. There was no casual pose with his hand in his pocket, no lopsided smile that welcomed me, no bag of Cheetos that may or may not be there.

There was just him, sprawled on the side of the road, the people around him watching him without knowing him, seeing his life slip away in minutes and seconds and blood. If he'd only stepped off the kerb a second later, we'd be on the way to the mall now, on the way to another adventure, away from all this mess.

But he was never late. He was always there.

Always there.

The Cheetos pendant burned against my chest and seared a hole through my skin—a glaring realization that Uncle Drew would never pick me up from school again.

* * *

'Oh my god. Can you not eat that in front of me? You're killing me here.'

I raise an eyebrow at him, and Uncle Drew shakes his head, grinning a translucent grin.

'You know what I mean,' he laughs.

'Have you even tried taking one?' I wave the freshly opened bag of Cheetos under his nose and he rolls his eyes. 'It might work, you know. If you want it bad enough.'

He scrunches up his face for a bit, then swipes his hand across the bag of chips. When his hand goes through the whole thing, he leans back in his chair across from me and groans.

I giggle and pop another cheesy sin into my mouth. He shakes his head.

'Now you're just showing off,' he says. 'You don't even *like* Cheetos.'

'People can change.' I do a quick survey of the tea shop to make sure we're still alone. 'Did I tell you Freyja's considering Ateneo now? She wants to be with Ryan so badly she's giving up her own dream.'

'And that is?'

'She's got her heart set on music school, which is actually something she's good at, and a school she can afford.' I shrug. 'This is why I choose to be single.'

'I don't think that's the reason at all.' Uncle Drew gestures around the shop. 'It's a Saturday night and you're sitting here in an empty tea shop with me instead of meeting boys in bars. Not that I want you to meet boys in bars. Where *do* you meet boys these days?'

'You've been gone three months, Uncle Drew. The world hasn't changed *that* much.' I smile at him. 'Besides, the buzz of the head cheerleader is behind me. I'm content with the simple and quiet life from here on out.'

'Riiight,' Uncle Drew strains his neck to peer at the empty counter. 'I'm sure the owner of this tea shop has nothing to do with your newfound appreciation for the quiet life.'

'He doesn't.' I check to make sure Luca is still in the back room before I go on. 'Do you know how many times I have flipped my hair over my shoulders around him? He doesn't care. Frankly, though, that's better for me. I don't need any distractions.'

'How admirable,' he smirks at me. 'Did you access my Google Drive yet, by the way?'

'No. You told me it was for emergencies only.'

'This can count as an emergency. There's a guy involved, right?' He grins, and I chuck a piece of Cheeto in his direction. It promptly goes through his laughing face. 'What about *your* college plans, Kali? Any campuses you're eyeing at the moment?'

'I got into three of them—'

'That's great!'

'—but I'm not going.'

'Oh.' He scratches his chin. 'Don't tell my sister that.'

'It just doesn't feel like it's right for me. Mom wouldn't understand.'

The sound of the back door creaking open makes me shoot out of my seat. I nod at Uncle Drew without a word and march back up the counter, and right on cue, Luca steps out with the resting frown that's probably etched permanently on his otherwise flawless face.

He stops in his tracks when he sees me. 'Oh. You're still here.' It's more of a statement than a question—I can tell his mind isn't fully here with me just yet, the wisps of his attention still inside those books in the back room. 'You don't have to stay,' he tells me. 'I'll lock up tonight.'

'No, it's okay—I'll do it.' I sneak a quick peek at the back room table where his books are scattered. In another less chaotic pile, a stack of notebooks sits nicely and neatly on the table. Each one is identically wrapped in a plain beige cover with nothing written on them, no inspirational quote in quirky font, no haphazard artwork of some kind of landscape, no electrifying graphic design. 'Um. What are you studying for, anyway?'

He blinks at me for a while before stroking the stubble on his chin. 'Board exam. Civil Engineering. I need to focus on this for now if I want to get anywhere.'

So *that's* why he hired me for some temporary help around here. 'Ah, I'm guessing you've got everything mapped out from here?'

'Pretty much.' He leans his back against the counter beside me, the stack of uniform notebook planners making much more sense. 'You?'

'I'm staying put. I kinda like not having to worry about the future.' My gaze flits over to the corner booth for a second. 'I mean, what's the rush, right?'

'Huh.' Luca crosses his arms. 'Living life on the edge, are we?'

'It's called stopping to smell the roses.' I reach out and run my fingers across the jars of tea leaves lined up on the shelf in front of us—it's the perfect way to keep my eyes from staring at how Luca's arms fill up his sleeves oh-so-nicely. 'Case in point: now that you're taking a break, you should have a cup of tea for a bit.'

Luca doesn't reply.

'Oh my god.' I drop my jaw and mock gasp at him. 'Have you even *tried* to drink our own milk tea?'

A flash of pink taints his cheeks for a bit, and it makes me want to mess with him even more.

'Alright, that's it.' I grab his arm and yank him away from the counter. I half expect him to jerk his arm back, but he surprisingly lets me lead him to the first table right in front of the counter. 'Sit.'

'Kali—'

'Sit. Down.'

He rolls his eyes and does as he's told, but I catch a small smile, which he's trying to bite back, dance across his lips for a second.

'You are going to sit there and let me make you some tea, and you're going to keep still for thirty minutes and enjoy it.'

'I—'

'No customers, no books. Just you and your tea, and whatever it is you like to think about when there are no distractions around.'

His eyes probe mine for a second too long, but then he blinks the tension away. 'Yes, ma'am.'

Half an hour later, I come back to clear his cup, and he sighs up at me in relief. He pushes his chair back and immediately makes a beeline for the counter, so I stomp right in front of him, and he hesitates.

'Nope.' I shake my head. 'You're not allowed to be in such a hurry to move on all the time. At least tell me how it was.'

'Torture, Kali. Torture.' He tries to scowl at me, but somehow, it turns into a small smile instead. 'Not the tea, though. Your tea was good.'

'That's all I asked.' I grin and step aside to let him pass, and he shakes his head with a small chuckle.

Progress.

He takes the cup from me and starts rinsing it in the sink. 'I hope there aren't more of these little experiments of yours down the road, Kali, or we might not make it through the next few weeks.'

'I can't promise anything,' I say. 'Tea for Two can use a little bit more life, to be honest.'

'Yeah?' He shakes the water off his hands and shuts the faucet, leaning against the sink to look at me. 'What did you have in mind?'

'I don't know—a two-for-the-price-of-one promo, a loyalty card, a seasonal drink. Even just a couple of posters here and there would do this place some good. Add a little bit of extra cheer.'

'Right.' Luca folds his arms across his chest again. 'Well, if you've got a few ideas, I'm open to them. I'm not cut out for this thing, to tell you the truth.'

I snap my fingers. 'Oh my god. I actually have a pretty good one. You don't hate music, do you?'

'No. I don't think anyone hates music.' He frowns. 'Do I . . . give off that impression?'

'No, of course not!' The words tumble out of my mouth in a hurry. 'Um, I just thought—you know . . . with all the books and stuff and the plain planners . . . I just thought you'd be, uh . . . '

'Boring?'

'No!' I turn red. 'Just . . . serious.'

Luca doesn't say anything else for a while, but the expression on his face twists into a knot that makes me wish I could just snap my fingers and take those past five seconds back.

He mutters something in a regional dialect I can't quite make out—Cebuano, maybe? I almost want to ask what he means, but thankfully, he clears his throat to wipe the odd look off his face in an instant. 'You were saying about music?'

'Um. Yeah. So,' I clear my throat too, 'my best friend is a musician, and she's *so* good, and I just thought maybe I'd ask her to come in and perform a few of her songs one afternoon, maybe like a random, impromptu live performance or something. We don't have to advertise or announce it or anything—she can just come in and do her thing. She's having a bit of a crisis lately, and I just think it's a good way to help her reignite the magic she's lost somehow.'

Luca doesn't say anything. My stomach lurches. 'Sorry. I know it might sound kinda selfish, and maybe it's not for the good of the cafe or anything, but I just think—'

'Sure.'

I jerk my head back. 'Sure?'

'Sure.' He shrugs. 'Could be fun. You're a good friend, Kali.'

I turn red again, but this time, it's because of a different pulse radiating from my chest. 'Cool. Thank you.'

We stand there staring at each other for a while, and I swear a corner of his lip almost tugs upward in another sideways smile. But then, he promptly swivels around and starts rinsing the cup in the sink again, even though I'm pretty sure it's already squeaky clean.

'So, uh,' I try to change the topic, 'are you planning to keep running this place after you get your license?'

'Tea for Two is only two months old.' He twists the faucet off and rakes a hand through his hair, messing it up even more. 'It's a summer gig. Just like yours.'

'What do you mean?'

At this, he raises an eyebrow at me, and his next words trample my so-called foolproof summer plan onto the cold, hard ground.

'I've only got a short-term contract here, Kali. The owner is taking this building down by the end of the month.'

Fate Is Fixed

The Colours He Took Away

Me

> Look what I got!

Me

> *[This message has been deleted.]*

Uncle Drew

> Wait, what? What happened

Uncle Drew

> Did you just send me a
> meme on Discord?

Uncle Drew

> I saw a photo

Me

> Okay so I was going to send you a picture
> of this XL Cheetos bag but decided to troll
> you instead with a photo of me grinning

Uncle Drew

I didn't see anything

Me

My internet sucks

Me

It's still spinning with this circle
icon thingy in the middle

Uncle Drew

Okay, well. Sucks to be you ha!

Me

BUT I'M THE ONE WITH THE CHEETOS

Uncle Drew

I'm coming over

The woman behind the last counter smiles at me after I say my thanks, but the smile I fire back somehow gets stuck halfway across my lips. There's nothing triggering about the posters I've just had printed in my hand—running this errand for Tea for Two's Buy One Get One promo was my idea in the first place—but today is just one of those days, and everything in the mall is suffocating.

Today is officially a Bad Day, especially since every single corner of the mall reminds me of Uncle Drew.

There's the Japanese katsu place with the all-you-can-eat shredded cabbage, where he and I once spent the whole afternoon chatting about . . . I don't even remember what we were chatting about. I was tinier then and was just tall enough to prop my arms properly on top of the table. I was seated across from him like a big girl, and how proud I was then that I could sit there and talk to him, just the two of us, like I was an adult and we had important matters to discuss.

I round a corner and there's the doorway that leads to the mall's al fresco area, where I used to run around squealing until, one day, I stepped on some dog poop because it's a pet-friendly mall, and Uncle Drew had to scrape the gross brown stuff off from under my favourite sneakers.

Down the escalator, my steps lead me right to this boutique shop where I spent the whole time we were in line at the cashier doing a trust fall and crashing into Uncle Drew's arms. Fast forward years later and it's the same boutique—me taking forever to pick out a pair of pants for a date and Uncle Drew falling asleep in one of the chairs by the dressing room.

Right outside is the long pathway that leads to the connecting bridgeway to the train station. As I speed through it with my head down low, I don't dare to look at the gaming shop off to the side where I once bought Uncle Drew credits for this mobile game he loved so much for his birthday.

The moment I step into the station, I take a deep breath to steady myself. It's not always this terrible, this ache in my heart that's scraping its way up my throat. I hobble to a quieter area where there's an open space for some fresh air, but all the stillness does is magnify the roaring in my chest.

The sun is setting, somehow. Commuters are scuffling off the platform and passengers are piling on the train, all this buzzing choked with movement and anger and frenzy and passion and life.

The world is spinning, still. It didn't stop when that car hit Uncle Drew, when he tried to look for me at the corner where we were supposed to meet for the last time, when he closed his eyes and never found me. Some days, I wonder if that driver ever thinks about what he's done, of the colours he took away, of how he stole what would've been a life of games and Cheetos and newsboy caps that never fade.

Most days, I realize that even knowing about it won't be enough.

My eyes sting. I'll never share a meal with Uncle Drew again, never gorge on unlimited cabbages or try on clothes with him melting of boredom in the corner. There are no birthday game credits or trust falls now and nobody around to catch me when I fall.

All I have now is Uncle Drew in the corner booth and this omnipresent fear that each time I talk to him might just be the last; that if I go to work the next day, he won't be there in the corner booth anymore. And that corner booth will be just what it is—a meaningless empty space.

I grip the posters in my hand a little tighter and swallow the hard lump in my throat, wading through the loneliness on my way to the ticket counters before the world moves on without me. The veil of grief weighs heavier for some reason. It extends a massive trail behind me—and I wear it like a corpse bride would, refusing to let go.

* * *

'I'm sorry to hear that, Kali.' -

Ryan always talks like he is a decade older than me, with his neatly gelled hair without a single strand out of place.

I keep telling him he's got his whole life to be this stuffy, boring adult he desperately wants to be, so he shouldn't be in a rush.

He leans back against the computer chair in my room that night, swivelling to look at me on my bed. 'Do we know what's going to happen to your uncle when they demolish the building?'

'I don't know.' I sigh, tapping the auto-battle function in the game on my phone. 'This isn't something that happens every day, you know?'

'Hmm, I'm assuming if that's his haunt then he may be stuck there in this plane, unable to leave.' He shrugs. 'At least, according to the movies.'

'We should probably ask some occult expert or something. Do we know anyone like that in our batch?'

'You should ask yourself, Kali.' Ryan swivels back around in my chair and starts tinkering around with my computer. 'You practically know the whole student body.'

It used to be so easy, breezing through high school where lights and colours would collide. It didn't take much—just me and my personality and the fact that I knew what I wanted and made sure I did everything I could to get it. 'A natural-born leader,' my teachers said, and before I knew it, I was at the top of the pyramid in my high ponytail and too-short skirt, cheering the jocks at games as the embodiment of the school spirit.

It was easy being in the limelight. I never shied away from it. Up there, I was comfortable. Up there, I belonged.

I was never mean, of course—I didn't want to be one of those Queen Bees the media always demonizes. My two best friends include an eccentric musician named after the

Norse goddess of love and sex but, in some versions, she's also the goddess of war and death. My other best friend happens to be said goddess' boyfriend, a straight-A student with his perfectly pressed shirt and his perfectly pleated pants, who is going to wow the world as the greatest lawyer humanity has ever seen.

Life was good. Life was simple. Life didn't have to mess it all up because of a four-word text message that brought my Uncle Drew to that corner at that time in that infinite bubble of eternity where Death caught up with him.

And it was all thanks to me. *Class ends at four.* I served him up on a platter for Death to savour, and Death owes me now, owes me forever.

I put my phone down and sigh. This private little corner of our house is a monument to my shame, a mausoleum of my grief. Mom and Dad are never around anyway, and I like it that way. They are always off to the next important business meeting that never ends, not when they think I'm fine, they think I'm okay. Not even when Uncle Drew died and all they did was host a funeral for him, all these flowers and pastries and messages that meant nothing then, mean nothing still.

How beautiful it must have been for them to spend all those years with him even before I was born, even when Uncle Drew was never one to colour within the lines, even when he left. The heartbreak my grandparents suffered through when he ran away, the realization that he never belonged and they never understood him. The anger the family stoked and fanned, until it consumed them all from the inside, until Uncle Drew never talked to them again.

How beautiful it must've been to let it all go when he died.

But a solemn burial and a meaningless ceremony later, Uncle Drew was gone, and all I had left was the broken mini-Cheetos bag around my neck and all the words I never got to say.

Until one day, I passed by Tea for Two and lingered in the corner where he breathed his last, and something inside caught my eye. A flash of a newsboy cap, a secret smile. The joy of times long past. The hope that the man who raised me while my parents were away was there, still right there, for me.

Uncle Drew was inside the tea shop, sitting in the corner booth as if he'd always been waiting for me.

Now that I've only got a month left, I'm not giving up. There has to be something I can do, something to keep the building from being condemned, something to keep him with me longer.

'I think I've got something.' Ryan's sudden voice jolts me back to the present. He types something into my keyboard then clicks on a website that has a bunch of names and some stats.

'Lay it on me.'

'A petition.' He rolls his shoulders, the glare from my computer screen shimmering on his glasses. 'You know how everyone's making Kickstarter campaigns for practically everything these days? Well, you can use the power of the internet—or the power of mob mentality—to your advantage.'

I bolt upright off my bed. 'Go on.'

'You can start an online petition and see how many signatures you can get to help save this thing.' Ryan points to a spot on my screen. 'Look. That building has always been a special after-school haunt for students, right? There aren't too many customers right now because school's out, and the tea shop is fairly new. But when classes are in full swing, it's always packed. It may have had different iterations over the years, but one thing remains the same—students flock to it because it's just a few steps away.'

I peer at the screen from behind Ryan. 'Do you think we can get enough signatures?'

'Sure. All we have to do is reach out to alumni and market the campaign on our social media accounts.' Ryan smiles at me. 'It's worth a shot, right?'

I scroll down and scan the different ongoing petitions on the site Ryan clicked on, all these people fighting for what they believe in and all these signatures backing them up with their cause. Mine might be a little selfish, but if it's going to help save something that's dear to the heart of other alumni, Ryan is right. It's definitely worth a shot.

Don't worry, Uncle Drew. I'm going to save you if it's the last thing I do.

* * *

When Uncle Drew was still alive, we used to bond over *Mitolohiya Mobile*, this mobile role-playing game where we'd spend forever trying to out-level each other. 'A five-star Tikbalang!' he'd brag to me, flaunting his dumb luck in getting rare characters in the game. 'A Bangungot!' 'A Sigbin!' 'All the top-tier units from the Aswang Clan!'

All I had were measly, low-level characters from the Diwata Clan, but he didn't want me to spend any real money to buy in-game currencies and stuff. Being a free-to-play player meant I had to get by with low-rarity weapons and ordinary characters. Earning enough to score an SSR character meant I had to grind away day after day, but I didn't mind—not when Uncle Drew was in the same boat (and in the same guild) as me.

His gig as a reviewer had its perks—I always got first dibs on codes and new video games he was offered, but I guess that was part of the reason why my grandparents thought he was wasting his life away. All they could see was him playing games all day—it's not like they could understand that he was just doing his job.

Now, though, it's just me alone with a sea of strangers in our guild, random usernames and Uncle Drew's character who would remain at his level forever. It doesn't seem fair that I get to embark on these raids and dungeon challenges without him, but giving up on the game altogether somehow means leaving everything we built behind.

So, here I am, still doing my dailies and trying to accomplish missions all by myself, struggling for some semblance of normalcy in a world that's turned upside down. And now that I get to see him and talk to him right across from me, I can't let anything get in the way, even if it means rallying to save a building from total destruction.

'I don't see how a simple petition can accomplish something like that,' Uncle Drew frowns, tilting his head to get a glimpse of the game on my phone. 'And what counts as a successful petition, anyway? How many signatures are you looking to collect?'

'Enough for people to take notice.' I toggle on the auto-battle function again, and my party of Diwata fairies—the equivalent of two knights, a priest, and a mage—starts battling endless hordes of demons on their own. 'You won't believe how much power a viral post holds, Uncle Drew.'

'I have a decent amount of followers on Instagram.' Freyja offers to help sitting beside me, smiling in Uncle Drew's general direction. She can't see or hear him, but she's somehow gotten the gist of the conversation from context clues. 'I don't mind promoting the petition. We'll get it done.'

Uncle Drew shoots my best friend a tentative smile. 'I know you girls are trying to help, Kali, but I don't think the followers of Freyja's music channel are going to care much about a random building they have no connection with.'

'And Ryan's got some pull too,' Freyja goes on, completely unaware of Uncle Drew's protests. 'He can work his magic in school.'

'Frey's right, you know. You gotta have a little faith—just leave the internet stuff to us.' I grin at him and he sighs just as the back door creaks to reveal an aloof Luca emerging from behind the counter.

I shift from my position in the corner booth when he shuffles toward me, his face all scrunched up. 'Kali, have you seen my digital tape measure anywhere? I can't seem to find it in the back room.'

'No, but I'll keep an eye out for it,' I snicker, and Freyja immediately straightens in her seat beside me. 'See, this is why I keep telling you to organize your stuff back there.'

A faint hint of pink sweeps across his face for a bit before he rubs his nape. 'Yeah.'

At the sight of the unfortunate tricep peeking out from under his white shirt, Freyja clears her throat and elbows my rib.

'Oh, Luca, this is Freyja. Freyja, Luca.'

Luca glances up from the floor and the corner of his lips tugs to the right. 'Oh. Hey. You'll be doing the live show in a few days, right?'

'Hi, and yes. Thanks again for having me.' Freyja flashes him her pearly whites. 'Kali didn't tell me her boss was this cute.'

'Frey!'

Luca looks confused for a bit before the front door opens with a tiny chime and Ryan saunters up to our booth. He takes one look at Freyja's teasing grin, my totally red face, and Luca standing there all awkward, and comes to his own conclusion with his lightning-fast wit.

'Hi, I'm Ryan.' He extends his hand out to Luca and gives it a firm shake. 'You must be Kali's boss?'

'Uh, yeah. Luca.' He still looks totally confused, the tint of pink on his cheeks growing warmer. 'I'd . . . better get back. Nice meeting you guys.'

He nods at Ryan and Freyja, averting his eyes from mine before heading back into the stockroom. As soon as he disappears, I stomp my foot as hard as I can on Freyja's.

'Ow! Kali!' She whines and giggles at the same time, and I spot Uncle Drew biting back a grin.

Even Ryan wiggles his eyebrows at me, and I roll my eyes. 'Aren't you both going to be late for your date or whatever it is you guys do without me?'

'Right.' Ryan flashes me a thumbs-up before leaning over to give Freyja a quick peck on the cheek. She gets up and winks at me before they both leave without another word.

I glare at Uncle Drew in their wake. 'Don't you dare.'

'What?' He shrugs. 'Even your best friends are thinking what I'm thinking. I'm on to something here, and maybe that's part of the reason you want to save this place so much.'

'It's *not*—I promise you that.' I focus back on my game and try my best to drive Luca's sheepish smile away from my mind. 'I'm going to save you if it's the last thing I do, Uncle Drew. I'm not going to lose you again.'

Maim My Heart One Last Time

Me

There's something new on my desk!

Uncle Drew

Yesssss

Me

Omigoshhh

Uncle Drew

Happy 8th birthday!

Me

When did you get these??? You sneaky

Uncle Drew

You were asleep. Little elves got the ponies and propped them up on your desk, all nice and ready for when you wake up.

Me

No wayyyy

Uncle Drew

You like them?

Me

Of course! Thanks, Uncle Drew!!!!!!!!!!

Uncle Drew

You're welcome, Kali Shandy.
Love you, kiddo

Me

😘

'For customer Carlisle?' I bark in my most barista voice to no one in particular. The tea shop is pretty much empty save for three small groups minding their own business at their own tables, but I still have to call out people's names from behind the bar like I'm fighting to be heard over the din of non-existent patrons. 'Customer Carlisle?'

I blink back my surprise when a teenage girl in an oversized shirtdress and scruffy Chucks walks up to me. 'That's me. Thanks.'

'One oolong tea latte with extra pearls, half sugar, no ice.' I hand her the medium-sized cup and grin. 'So, Carlisle, huh?'

She grimaces. 'Yeah. Mom was super into *Twilight*.'

'Sure, but Carlisle for a girl? That's new. Derivative, but new.'

'I know,' she sighs. 'Don't tell my mom that.'

'If it helps, I know someone in my class named Bella Edward. You got off easy.'

'When you put it that way.' She grins and raises her milk tea at me. 'Thanks.'

'Anytime,' I say, and she walks off just as Luca reappears from the back room. I catch the not-so-subtle double-take she gives my elusive boss right before she settles down in the corner booth away from my view. I wonder how Uncle Drew feels each time customers converge in the corner booth.

'You're really good at that,' Luca nods at me while refilling the straws.

I turn my body to face him. 'At what?'

'The small talk. Something I dread like a plague.' He indulges me with a small smile. 'Like I said. I'm not cut out for this job.'

Given how he's acting, I guess we're both going to pretend my so-called best friend's inappropriate comment a few days ago never happened. I'm cool with that. 'I was head cheerleader. I guess you learn a thing or two when you're on top.'

And, as if right on cue, the aforementioned BFF shuffles into Tea for Two with her head down and her guitar case in her hand. Freyja slogs right up to me and Luca in front of the counter, radiating a bundle of nerves so frazzled she zaps my nerves to a crisp.

'I can't believe I'm doing this.' She grits her teeth at me. 'Why did I ever let you talk me into it?'

'Because you're named after the goddess of war and death.' I plant both hands on her shoulders. 'You'll blow everyone away. Besides, there's only, what, like, ten people in here? No offence, Luca.'

'None taken.' Luca shrugs and offers Freyja a reassuring smile. 'You'll do great.'

I know he's only trying to be nice, as he's never even heard Frey play before, but it's still worth it just to see that hint of positivity on his face. 'What Luca said,' I say. 'Whenever you're ready.'

Freyja takes a long enough breath for me to think about her literally blowing everyone away. But then she bends down, unclasps her instrument from her case on the floor, and slings the strap over her head. When she plucks a few strings to tinker around with her tuning, a few people's heads start turning toward her, so Luca and I retreat behind the counter to keep her in the spotlight.

I haven't prepared any kind of introduction because I want Frey to feel like this is just a random session with her and her guitar—no big audience, no build-ups, no pressure whatsoever. Besides, if I want her to rediscover her love for her music, it should be in a setting that's as intimate as this.

Interestingly, everyone in the cafe suddenly gravitates toward her, leaning forward on their tables or turning their heads around at her in anticipation. Freyja doesn't look up at the small crowd, doesn't review their faces, doesn't introduce herself. She just closes her eyes and I know she's retreated into her own world where there's only her music and her words and nothing else.

And, finally, she sings.

You said that maybe this was for the best.
But maybe you didn't see the scar in my chest.
The wound that split open as it cracked and it grew.
The moment you smiled like you already knew.

You said that maybe you weren't the one,
That maybe love wasn't kind to the course we'd run.
But maybe you don't remember how I wanted to be.
Everything you were searching for if only you'd let me.

I bite back a smile as I watch my best friend enrapture the whole cafe with her performance. She quivers every word in soft tones, her heart throbbing through every part of the lyric, and as she strums her calloused fingers on her lonely strings, I see Carlisle shoot up from her booth in the corner and start filming Freyja on her phone.

So before you go, before you go,
Could you tell me I was worth it just so I would know?
Before you go, before you go,
Could you give me back our memories to soften the blow?

So before you go, before you go,
Could you tell me what I should've said to keep the flame aglow?
Before you go, before you go,
Could you maim my heart one last time so I'd have something to show?

For some reason, something hot and thick starts pushing against my eyelids. I blink the enchantment away and scan the cafe to see just how spellbound everyone is. But when my eyes land on Luca beside me, I realize he's not even looking at Frey.

He's looking at me.

There's a glassy veil shielding his eyes at the moment, and it kills me that I can't figure out what he's thinking. He doesn't say anything for a while, so I swallow the lump in my throat. 'Her music is beautiful, isn't it?' I whisper.

Luca doesn't reply, but then Freyja ends her song with a flourish and everyone starts clapping, breaking whatever trance Luca seems to be in. He turns away from me then, mumbling something out of earshot.

I swear I caught him say the word 'beautiful' under his breath.

'KALI!' Frey launches into a bear hug and leaps right at me behind the counter, frantic and breathless. 'Did you hear that? DID YOU?'

I giggle amid the tangle of Freyja's wild hair and her even wilder energy. 'Yes! Oh my god, Frey—'

'I did it!' Freyja squeezes even tighter. 'That was . . . that was just—'

'Magic.' Luca offers beside us, and without warning, Freyja untangles herself from me and wraps Luca in a bear hug too. He freezes and just as randomly as she hugged him, she lets him go. 'You, sir, have earned a huge check in my book.'

'Uh—'

'Okay, I'm off! Thanks, Kal—love you!' Just like that, Frey grabs her case and saunters right out of Tea for Two, taking all the fire and electricity with her.

Luca's still frozen solid where Frey left him, and it almost makes me burst out laughing.

'That's Freyja.' I giggle. 'Thank you for letting her play.'

'Um. Yeah. No problem.' He finally thaws himself. 'She's good. She's planning on taking up music in college?'

I sigh. 'That's the thing, though, I don't think she wants to, which is a waste. When you've got talent that good, it just seems like such an obvious choice.'

Luca leans against the row of jars across from me. 'What about *your* choice, Kali? Why aren't you going on campus tours like you ought to?'

I don't reply for a while, because after that spectacular display of Freyja's talent, it dawns on me even more cruelly that I don't have as clear a vision as she does.

'Because I don't want to.'

'Taking a year off?'

'Maybe.'

'Plans?'

'I'm not sure.' I shrug. 'Maybe . . . maybe I'll stay here.'

Luca folds his arms across his chest, and I peek down at his toned arms for the briefest millisecond. 'Kali. You do understand what "demolished" means, right?'

'This place isn't getting demolished. Not if I can help it.' I fish my phone from my apron pocket and show him my campaign. 'I started a petition.'

'To save this place?' Luca takes the phone from me and our fingers touch. He doesn't seem to notice. 'Why would anyone want to do that?'

'Because. It's a cultural landmark, this place.' I try to shake off his electric touch on my skin. 'I mean, it's where alumni used to hang out all the time. These walls have memories.'

'These walls have cracks, probably. Not that I've checked.' Luca frowns at my screen. 'I mean, don't get me wrong,

I'll totally support you on this. But it just feels like you have too much time on your hands.'

I brush my fingers over the Cheetos pendant on my chest. 'Maybe.'

He sighs. 'Look. I need to drop off some stuff at school tomorrow afternoon. You want to come with?'

I straighten up. 'To UST?'

'Yeah,' he shrugs. 'I can give you a quick tour around the campus. You might change your mind about taking a year off, and it'll give you something to do.'

The idea of spending the day with Luca outside of cafe grounds is intriguing to say the least. Besides, he doesn't seem to think there's anything weird about him practically asking me out on a date. 'Um, yeah. Sure. Why not?'

'Cool. I'll pick you up.' He types his number into my phone before handing it back to me, and this time, his fingers linger on mine for just a second longer. Or is it just my imagination? 'Text me your address.'

'Okay.' I send him my details like it's no big deal, like my heart isn't fluttering and my stomach isn't churning with each letter I type. 'So, you're leaving Tea for Two closed tomorrow?'

At this, he swallows heavily, making me zero in on the smooth curves of his Adam's apple, which I have never noticed before. His grey eyes bore into mine. 'I'm not glued to this place, Kali. Not when there are more important things to do.'

* * *

As soon as the group of girls punctuates their performance with a final fist pump, my arm twitches. My instincts are almost telling me to join this buzzing mass of strangers as they clap to signal the end of cheerleader practice in the middle of the field. With the way they're slapping each other on their backs, all smiles and sweat and pure elation, this familiar twitch in my chest pulses.

The electricity is infectious, but all that's behind me now. There's no more space for plastering on of smiles and leading of cheers in my future—all that's left is the ghost of a wayward uncle and his month-long time limit.

'Kali!'

Luca's sharp tone wrenches my attention away from the girls in front of me with such force that my head whips in his direction. To my right, Luca's crossing the greenery with his hands in his pockets, looking very much in his element out here without the barista backdrop behind him.

'Hey.' He sits down on the stone bench beside me, running a hand through the mess of curls on his forehead. 'Sorry it took a while. The registrar was being all kinds of difficult.'

'No biggie.' I tilt my head toward the cheerleaders packing up on the field in front of us. 'I had some entertainment.'

'Ah. Right.' He stretches and casually drapes an arm around the back of the bench we're on. If I didn't know how disinterested Luca was, I'd think he was making a move. 'Another reason you might want to reconsider not going to college.'

'To join the pep squad?' I shake my head, the space between his arm and my back tingling with imagined electricity. 'I think my cheerleading days are over.'

'Or you could be a student volunteer with the registrar. No use putting your skilled small talk to waste. They could use a little sunshine over there.'

'Ha ha.' I roll my eyes at him and he actually gives me a small sideways smile. He doesn't say anything else after that, and the silence fires up all these possibilities in my head—dangerous thoughts that range from Luca calling me sunshine to the image of us sitting on the bench like this in the middle of campus, me in that perilous space nestled between his body and the crook of his arm.

Luca didn't say much on the car ride here after he picked me up, but he didn't have to. Somehow, we both settled into an easy silence with only my thoughts wandering into uncharted territory. I never know what they're called, but Luca's car is one of those adorable hatchbacks that doesn't have too much space inside. With me in the passenger seat, it felt cosy rather than cramped—the kind where his hand would've brushed against mine whenever he shifted gears if I wasn't careful.

The tension—or, at least, the tension *I* felt—dragged on until after he parked and he was leading me down the narrow lot, his gentle hand lightly pushing against the small of my back. We were almost out of the steel parking when I remembered I'd left my phone charging in his glove compartment. So, of course, I whipped around so suddenly that my face smacked right into his chest.

His unfortunately tough, unfortunately Luca chest.

He acted like it was no big deal, offered to run back to the car to grab my phone for me, and proceeded with his own version of a campus tour. It didn't help that a few people said hi to him from afar. I could only imagine what must have been going through their minds, seeing him strolling through campus with me by his side. Then, he stopped by the registrar to do what he came here to do, and now here we are.

All this touching-but-not-touching is derailing me from my single-minded mission, but I can't afford any distractions for the rest of the month.

Luca shifts his position and leans forward, resting his elbows on his knees. He peers up at me through his long lashes then, with an expression that definitely counts as a distraction. 'You hungry?'

Something inappropriate zips through my mind, but I shake it off. 'I don't want to keep you. I'm good.'

'Well, I am. Let's go grab something to eat.'

'Okay.'

I bite my lip. For whatever reason, he seems determined to prolong this not-a-date with me, and if it means getting to spend more time with him like this, I'm not going to complain.

Luca leads me out the small pedestrian gate to one side of the campus, and we cross the street to a three-table ramen house. It's nothing fancy—just a black and red motif and a five-item menu that suits Luca's no-nonsense personality perfectly. There are no other customers at the moment, and as Luca picks the table near the far end of the shop, he even pulls out my chair for me.

And they say chivalry is dead.

'The shoyu ramen is out of this world, but it's going to ruin our appetites for dinner.' Luca shrugs, but my mind fixates on the word 'dinner' and refuses to move on. 'The takoyaki is divine too, though.'

As soon as I gape at the photo of the shoyu ramen on the menu, all thoughts of not wanting to keep him promptly catapult out the window. My stomach groans. 'Oh my god. That does look like heaven.'

'Yeah?' Luca eyes me from the top of his own menu. 'We can split one if you want.'

Um. What.

I swallow. 'Are you sure?'

He shrugs. 'Why not? Shame if I brought you here and you didn't get to try the specialty.'

'Okay. Yeah. Sure.' I'm seeing a completely different side of my normally indifferent boss today, and it's almost as if taking this elusive creature out of the tea shop habitat has somehow changed his spots.

I'm one to talk, though. I've never had a problem being the more forward one when it comes to the opposite sex in school. But with Luca, I'm an awkward bundle of nerves. I guess I don't do too well when taken out of my habitat too.

Luca exchanges pleasantries with the waitress, and it's clear that he's a regular here. I try to ignore how the female staff smile at him in a way that's too close for comfort, because what the heck am I even squirming about?

He's my boss. I'm his temporary employee. It's not like those kinds of relationships ever have a happy ending.

When the steaming ramen arrives and as soon as I take my very first slurp, my eyes flutter shut. 'Oh my god.'

Luca smiles at me then—an actual, genuine, full smile. 'After that and the tour, I take it you're considering college again?'

'Yes. No. Maybe.' *If I do choose to go here, it's not like you'll be around with me.* 'I'm in no rush to move things along.'

'So I've heard.'

I smirk at him. 'It's called being in the present, which is something you should learn to do.'

'Right. Stopping to taste the milk tea and all that.' He smirks back. 'So you're a mindfulness expert now?'

'No, but I do yoga. Gotta keep this cheerleader bod flexible, you know? You should do it with me sometime.'

Luca almost chokes on his soup.

'Yoga! I mean, do yoga with me.' I turn beet red, but it helps that Luca's face has turned a shade of pink too. 'Um. You know. Do yoga. With me. Learn to be in the present and slow down and stuff.'

For the longest second ever, I almost imagine him straight-up leaving me with a vehement 'nope', but then he averts his eyes and is suddenly transfixed by a spot behind my right ear. He clears his throat. 'Uh, sure. That'd be pretty cool.'

'Okay. Cool.' I parrot him, opting to train my eyes on the wall behind him too. My gaze hovers from there to an awkward little stain on the table between us, then it settles somewhere around a cosy nook on Luca's throat and refuses to leave.

We focus on our half-ramens for a while without saying anything, the bowls of comfort adding to the glow of this moment in time. Maybe I'll look back on this one day and wonder why I didn't try to keep Luca with me for as long as I could, or I'll realize with a pleasant surprise how I could still remember exactly the way the table we shared felt like home.

'Why *do* you want to take a year off?' He leans back in his chair and swallows, drawing my eyes further into the curve of his neck. 'Why do you want to stay at the shop so badly?'

For a second I consider telling him everything, but I think about the privacy of Uncle Drew's haunt and what might happen if Luca started minding the corner booth. 'Like I said. It's a cultural landmark.'

'And that concerns you, why?'

'Call me nostalgic.'

He eyes me again with that steely look in his greyish eyes, and it almost feels like he's behind the counter at Tea for Two again. But then he blinks and the softness is back. 'Look, if you don't feel like telling me, that's fine. All I'm saying is, don't knock it till you've tried it. College will give you the most beautiful memories you won't want to forget.'

At this, I finally find my inner Kali and wave my hand at the space between us. 'Like this?'

Luca doesn't say anything for a while, but he doesn't take his eyes off me, either. The tips of my ears start tingling with a sudden warmth, but this time, I don't avert my gaze.

Which is how I catch his eyes flickering down to my lips for the briefest millisecond.

'Yes, Kali,' he finally says. 'Exactly like this.'

* * *

The text message that lights up my entire room that night bathes what happened this morning in an even softer glow. The day, rose-coloured and impossible, almost feels like a separate bubble of giddiness, like that scene in a movie where a montage of dates plays out while an upbeat song about hearts and kisses bops along in the background.

'Thanks for coming with today.' Luca's text drowns out everything else in my already empty house. 'Can I take you up on your offer?'

> **Me**
>
> Yoga?

Luca

> Yeah. Is that okay?

> **Me**
>
> Just say when.

Luca

> Tomorrow morning?

I bite my lip. A session in the morning only means we'll be stuck with each other all afternoon once my shift starts at four, and if it goes badly, the next five hours cramped behind the counter with Luca will be torture.

But if it goes well . . .

My fingers can't type fast enough.

> **Me**
>
> Wear comfy clothing. And NO distractions.

I don't think I've ever fixated on those three dots this much.

Luca

> I'm all yours.

White Noise Between Us

Fire_Drewid

Guild war in 10 minutes

KaliShandy88

Whatttt I'm not ready

Fire_Drewid

No one is ready for the wrath of the gods

KaliShandy88

Am I supposed to be at your beck and call? I'm 18, Uncle Drew. What if I'm on a date

Fire_Drewid

You're not

KaliShandy88

What if I am??????

Fire_Drewid

Then he joins our noble quest or you ditch him

KaliShandy88

OMG you're lucky I'm single

KaliShandy88

And I'm still missing those last three tasks

KaliShandy88

If I don't get this platinum shield set

Fire_Drewid

I'll farm the materials for you.

KaliShandy88

I swear, Uncle Drew

Fire_Drewid

I got your back, Kali.

Fire_Drewid

Always.

The instant I hear Luca's car pulling up in the driveway, my stomach knots into something totally unbecoming of a Queen Bee who usually knows what she's doing. Having the whole house to myself with parents who are never home has its perks in high school, but with Luca, somehow it feels like I shouldn't be trusted to be all alone with him.

My gut feel is right, though, because as soon as I open the front door, the sight of Luca in sweatpants already catapults all my defences out the window.

'Hey,' he grunts, shifting his weight from one foot to the other.

'Hey.' I smile, and he raises an arm to rub the back of his neck. 'Welcome to my humble abode.'

He scans the living room as soon as I close the front door behind him, then shakes his head. 'You weren't kidding when you said your parents are never home.'

'I wasn't. Shall we?'

He nods curtly, and I lead him through the kitchen and up the stairs to my room, where I've laid out two yoga mats side-by-side on the floor. I settle down barefoot on one of them then notice him hesitating by the door.

There's a faint shade of pink on his cheeks, and I'd like to think my tank top and leggings (that hug my body oh-so-perfectly) have something to do with it.

I gesture to the mat beside me. 'It's clean—don't worry about it.'

'That's not what I—' His face grows redder, then he clears his throat. 'Okay.' He settles down beside me and mimics my position on the mat. 'You should know I've never tried this before, so go easy on me.'

I spend the first few minutes teaching him how to breathe properly—the real, conscious kind of breathing—but even that proves to be a challenge for him. Luca obviously doesn't know the concept of being in the moment, seeing how he keeps fidgeting in discomfort every few seconds.

By the time we get to his first Child's Pose, a full-on frown has carved itself onto his face.

'Now, inhale, push up to a table position then lay your hands flat on the mat and gently stretch back to Downward Facing Dog.' I glance at him as he tries to emulate my position with a grunt, and I snicker.

'Don't try to fight it so much—it's not the end of the world.'

'*Ahh samuka,*' he grits his teeth, and, to my surprise, chuckles. 'My body isn't made for this kind of thing.'

I giggle and get up from my position. 'Sure it is—you just need a little practice is all. It's not rocket science.' I step onto his mat. 'Look—right here. You just need to adjust your hips and—'

I lay my hands on either side of his lower back, but the instant I make contact, he jerks sideways like I just burned him. His whole body collides right into me and we both lose our footing. He crashes on his back on the mat.

And I land right on top of him.

We stay frozen in place on my bedroom floor, my whole body squished on top of his, the two of us panting and staring at each other, me very much aware that my bed is literally inches away from where we are. My eyes zero in on the beads of sweat that disappear down his neck, and I let my mind wander for one dangerous second to imagine how it would feel to see that kind of sweat on Luca for . . . other reasons.

The moment stretches out into infinity, the heat in my room searing through every single second. But then I feel Luca's hands grab my waist with a special kind of urgency as he *lifts* my whole body off him and rolls me off to the side. He scrambles up off the mat and clenches his fist, refusing to look at me.

'Sorry, uh, we should call it a day.'

I tuck my knees under my legs on the mat and try to calm my own heart, feeling bolder somehow and finding the old Kali in me again for the briefest second. 'You can't give up yet.' This is my turf, after all, and seeing Luca all frayed along the edges is giving me the confidence boost I need. 'It's okay, Luca—everyone falls the first time.'

He hesitates for a while, but then a small smile flits across his lips for a second before he clears his throat. 'So, I haven't blown my chances just yet?'

I grin at him. 'We're just getting started.'

* * *

I stride into Tea for Two a lot cheerier than usual that afternoon, and Uncle Drew immediately calls me out on it.

'I know *that* look.' He grins at me as soon as I slide into his corner booth. 'Been seeing your boss outside office hours lately?'

'First of all, ick, Uncle Drew.' I roll my eyes to feign nonchalance, but I'm pretty sure my cheeks are on fire. Just because we tell each other everything doesn't mean I want my uncle to be privy to my love life or lack thereof. 'Second, it was just a tour around his campus.'

'A school-sanctioned tour?'

'No, but—'

'With no extracurricular activities right after?'

'Well—'

'There you go.' His grin grows wider. 'Love is a thunderstorm, kiddo.'

'Yeah, yeah.' I wave a hand between us, then fish my phone out of my pocket to change the subject. 'The petition is doing fab, by the way. Just so you know, I'm still hell-bent on keeping you here.'

At this, a sigh instantly wipes out the grin on Uncle Drew's face. 'Thanks, Kali. It's not that I'm not grateful for your efforts, but are you sure this is the most productive use of your spare time?'

'I can't imagine doing anything else.' I lean over and scroll through my petition page, showing him the signatures that have now reached a little under fifty. I watch as his ghostly eyes scan the names he doesn't know, his face all scrunched up.

'This reminds me of that time when you were six.' He leans back in his chair and rubs a finger over his temple. 'You kept showing me this cartoon cloud thing on your iPad, rewinding the thing over and over because you found the character's line funny.'

'Adventure Time!' I shove my phone back into my pocket and snicker. 'Lumpy Space Princess is the boss.'

'Right. The purple princess.' Uncle Drew shakes his head. 'You kept repeating her line about parties or some such when all I wanted was to take a nap that afternoon. You parroted that line so much it was stuck in my head for a week.'

I giggle. 'And this is like that, how?'

'I *mean*,' he gestures around us, 'that this is clearly important to you, and I'm all for it. I'm happy here, kiddo, and I'm glad I get to spend this time with you. But don't you think you're rewinding something to death instead of just . . .

you know.' He holds himself back, almost like he's afraid of how I'd react. 'Instead of just moving on.'

And just like that, whatever chirpy mood I was in when I came in zips away. I grit my teeth. 'Easier said than done.'

'Dropping the petition?'

'No,' I look him in the eye. 'Moving on.'

'Kali.' Uncle Drew reaches his hand out to me then, like he could actually hold me, like he could offer anything else but his transparent presence. 'I want to be here as much as you do, but are you sure you're okay?'

'I am. I've got this petition to focus on, don't I?' I withdraw my hand from the table, almost forgetting that Uncle Drew can't hold his hand over mine, anyway. 'If you're worried about me moving on, this is it. This is how I can move on.'

'By keeping all this from your family?'

'You kept your life from yours too.'

'It's not something you should model your future after.'

'You practically raised me,' I snap. 'It's only natural.'

'Kali—'

'Look, I don't want to argue with you, all right?' I stand and Uncle Drew's eyes rise up with me, defeated. 'I have to get to work.'

I stomp to the counter with my fist balled, like digging my nails into my palm would keep the tears from falling. There's a lump in my throat that I force down with a deep swallow. That veil of grief normally just floats around me on good days, but it rears its ugly head on occasion. I'm not going to let this be a Bad Day.

I take a deep breath to steady the growing weight in my chest as I lay a hand on the doorknob of the back room.

When I feel like myself again, I clear my throat and turn the handle.

As expected, Luca's bent over his desk with his books scattered all around him, his face hidden behind his laptop.

'Hey,' I greet him. 'You okay?'

'Hey. Yeah.' Luca looks up at me and his lips twist into a small smile, but something stops him midway. Instead, his face contorts into this awkward expression that makes him look like he just ate some bad shrimp. The conflicted look lingers on his face for a while then he promptly returns to his books without saying anything else.

I try to squash the twinge of disappointment in my chest. So we had two mornings outside of work together—no big deal. It's not like I should be expecting him to be all chummy with me now.

'Um, so, I'll just be out here,' I mumble to the space above his head, and he doesn't even reply. Now that he's back in his natural habitat, the frustratingly odd creature that is Luca is now back to . . . whatever this is.

I bite back a sigh and drag my feet out to the counter, but as soon as I step out of the back room, Luca's chair scrapes against the floor with a screeching urgency.

I whip back around and he's leaning against the door frame now, staring down at me still with that bad-shrimp look on his face.

'Luca?'

'I . . . ' He shoves a hand in his pocket and sighs. 'I need to do a quick supply run.'

'Oh. Okay, sure. I can hold the fort for you.'

'What? No, I—' He shifts from one foot to another. The stud earring on his ear glistens underneath the flattering bar lights.

'I want you to come with me,' he finally blurts out, clenching his jaw like that line was one of the most difficult things he's ever had to say. 'Is that okay?'

He bites his lip, and I get this sudden urge to nibble on it myself.

Crap.

* * *

The air hums with something else inside Luca's car this time around. While I was absolutely sure I was the only one losing my mind over the imagined sparks between us in his car yesterday, today is an entirely new beast.

For one thing, Luca hasn't let his hand casually drop to his side during the whole car ride. He's been gripping the steering wheel like a man possessed, and I'm pretty certain it's to make sure he doesn't accidentally brush his hand against mine.

For another, the easy silence from yesterday is all gone now, replaced by some kind of oppressive tension that's killing me one stoplight at a time.

As for what kind of tension this is, well, I still have to figure that out.

When we stop at the nth traffic light, Luca grumbles his first word to me since I got into the passenger seat. 'Sorry.'

I tilt my head at him. 'For what?'

'The gridlock,' he motions at the road ahead of us. 'I didn't expect traffic to be this bad.'

'It's okay,' I shrug and scramble to be myself again. 'I like being in the car with you.'

He tosses me a sideways glance I can't quite read, then combs a hand through his hair, finally easing up a bit. 'I only need a couple of things, but the line is always impossible. I just need a wingman for a bit.'

I don't know why he's explaining himself when it's only normal that I help him with these things. It's my job, after all. 'Don't worry about it. I'm a great wingman. Just ask Frey and Ryan.' I smack my lips together and notice him glancing down at my mouth again. My stomach squirms. 'How did you come by Tea for Two while prepping for your board exam, anyway? Can't your parents help you out or something?'

'My parents are in Cebu.' The light flickers green, and he averts his eyes from my face to the road ahead. 'They can't exactly lend me a hand if they'll need a plane ride to get here.'

'So, why the extra workload?'

'I need to keep moving. I just need this for a few weeks until I pass and get a job.'

I fold my arms across my chest and grin. 'No wonder I never see you hanging out with your friends.'

'None of them are taking the boards yet, not straight out of graduation.'

'Is that so wrong? Pacing yourself?'

He eyes me again. 'It's a luxury I can't afford.'

I pause and expect him to expound, but I guess that's all he's willing to say about that. It's obvious his situation with his parents isn't exactly ideal, but who am I to judge? Mine isn't all sunshine and butterflies, either.

Now the reason why he's encouraging me to go to college makes a lot more sense. It's the next step in life, and for Luca, he's obviously all about keeping things moving.

Which, unfortunately, is the complete opposite for me.

We park at a little side street across a wholesale grocery shop a little while later, and as soon as I get out of Luca's car, I can already spot the flood of people closing in on the front entrance. Customers spill out onto the sidewalk like littered candy, and we both squeeze our way through to a window off to one side.

'Here.' Luca pulls a ticket stub with a number on it from the window, then hands me a sheet of paper with a list of what we need. 'I need you to submit this when they call your number. I'll be at the back—I just need to sort out a couple of things with the delivery staff.'

'Sure. No problem.'

He nods his thanks at me and disappears into the crowd. I clutch the ticket stub and the material list to my chest. There are just too many people here, every single human being restless and fuming. I try to find a quiet corner to myself that's still within earshot just in case whoever's supposed to call out my number does just that, but there's no empty space here, no small haven or respite for a newbie like me.

I swallow. Someone bumps into me from behind, and I shimmy away elsewhere to keep moving with the crowd. Whipping out my phone to pass the time doesn't seem like a good idea either, as I'll probably lose it in the oblivion as soon as the crowd shifts.

I shuffle along and squeeze my way through each time a small space opens up, and I think I make it a full half hour before it happens.

The shove. As expected from this powder keg of agitation, one wrong move sends the whole crowd rippling into indignant outcries and wanton pushing. Somewhere, somehow, some punk rams into someone else a little too passionately, and the wave cascades over me too quickly for me to react.

The deluge of people in front of me lose their footing and trip backwards, sending me toppling back right along with them. A helpless yelp scrambles up from my chest and stops midway through my throat because just as I expect to fall flat on my ass, a pair of arms cushions my fall.

Instead of the cold hard concrete, my back lands smack into the warmth of Luca's body as he tugs at my tiny frame and relieves me from the chaos.

'Are you okay?' His low voice against the back of my ear rumbles through every frayed nerve, and before I can even respond, he leads me to a corner and firmly plants both his hands against the wall on either side of my head.

Pinned against the wall with Luca right in front of me, I lose my voice completely.

'Sorry—I shouldn't have left you,' he whispers, looking over his own shoulder at more pushing and pulling behind him. I'm still trying to piece together why he's using his body to shield me from the crowd, when a violent jostle shoves him even closer to me, my face now barely inches from the inviting curves of his neck.

For a second, the heat of the crowd singes into the heat of something else, and the sight of Luca's exposed throat right in front of my lips makes me forget everything and everyone. I'm so mesmerized by our proximity that I lay a hand on his chest, and the light contact makes Luca turn away from the crowd behind him and stare down at my face.

The seconds stretch out into eternity. His breath tickles. I can't tell if I'm imagining his heart speeding up under my palm, but I swear he leans down and inches his face closer.

I tilt my chin up.

And somebody calls our number.

Luca practically propels himself off the wall away from me, his face all kinds of red. He takes the ticket stub from my hand and his fingers leave a singed trail on mine in their wake.

I'm in a daze as we process the payment, sign the delivery forms, and get back in the car. Luca doesn't say anything else, but he doesn't have to—the buzzing white noise between us says it all.

Today is a confession of sorts, and our own bodies have just betrayed us both.

Love Is a Thunderstorm

I Can Show You if You Like

Frejya plucks an imaginary string of her air guitar then holds her fingers out in front of her like she's inspecting a fresh manicure. She hasn't said a word for a full fifteen minutes now, which, given that there's no screaming kid flailing in the pool in front of us, makes the silence in her condo common area more oppressive.

I normally don't have a problem with days like these, but something deep inside my belly has been twisting and writhing and buzzing for the past few days, and I've been debating telling Frey all about it.

Obviously, though, she's got something just as oppressive on her mind at the moment, hence the incessant imaginary music-making. And I know Frey well enough to let her ease into the convo herself rather than pry.

My phone buzzes to life on my lap. I peek at the message preview.

Luca.

But just as I'm about to swipe the message open with the enthusiasm of a kid in a candy store, Freyja finally sighs.

'Ryan is an ass.'

I put my phone down. 'Sure.'

'He thinks I should give up on Ateneo.' Freyja clenches her fist, any semblance of her delicate air-strumming gone. 'It's like he doesn't even want to spend college together.'

'You can't get in anyway, right?' I shift my position on the bench to face her. 'Didn't you say you can't afford it?'

'I can still go for the instalment plan,' she says. 'There are ways out if you want something this badly.'

'Do you, though?'

She frowns at me. 'What's that supposed to mean?'

I sigh. Does this mean that whole performance at Tea for Two meant squat? 'Do you really want to go to Ateneo? You can't pursue your music there, right? I mean, you're practically giving up your dream just to be with Ryan.'

'Music is a *hobby*, Kal. You can't expect me to live off of that right after graduation.'

'Yeah, but shouldn't you at least try? Don't you owe it to yourself?'

'It's not that simple,' she says. 'It's not just about being on the same campus as Ryan. Music is a fairy-tale, and if I'm being honest with myself, I'll need a proper degree—from a really good university—to even attempt to support it.'

'That's such a negative way to look at it. Maybe ask your parents? You haven't even tried and you're already giving up.'

'I'm not.' Freyja clenches her jaw now. 'I *have* to look way ahead into the future—mine and Ryan's. I can't just stay here in this little bubble of make-believe where friendship is magic and music is life. We don't *all* have the luxury of studying abroad or choosing to stay put because our finances are pretty much covered for eternity.'

At this, she grips the edge of the bench we're on and widens her eyes at me. I don't think she even realizes what she just said, but the damage is done.

'Kali, I—'

'I'm late for work.' I grab my phone and stand, but Freyja just sits there with a wounded look in her eyes. She doesn't say anything else as I leave the condo, but she doesn't have to. Deep down, I know she's right.

I'm staying put in this so-called bubble to save Uncle Drew and keep him where he is, keep things as they are. I'm choosing to take a year off because I want to, but more importantly, because I can. College will be waiting for me, here or with my aunt in Texas.

But as privileged as that sounds, I can't afford to falter here either.

My world already stopped when Uncle Drew died—I can't move on without him.

* * *

The day twists into something less defined, more blurred around the edges. Luca's text turned out to be just a simple enquiry about whether I was coming in for work, but it was merited—some magic of the weather waved its way into Tea for Two somehow this afternoon and it was packed as soon as I arrived.

I've been manning the counter all day without the slightest chance to slide on over to Uncle Drew's booth, which probably is a good thing, looking back. I didn't particularly leave things all fine and dandy with him the last time we spoke, and with Freyja's words dragging me down like an unwanted weighted blanket, it's suffocating.

Luca has been weaving in and out of the counter today. Having him so close in this too-cramped space behind the bar doesn't make breathing any easier, not when we both know what happened—or didn't happen—the last time our bodies almost touched among a densely packed crowd.

The heat won't stop searing through my nerves each time he gets too close.

By the time the last customer finally steps out of the shop, the streetlights outside have already begun casting the summer evening in a warmer, softer glow. Luca flips the sign on the door, lays his flawlessly folded apron on the front counter, and sighs.

I take one look at the perfectly folded square and start our first conversation of the day. 'How is this even possible?'

At the sound of my normal, non-barista voice, he finally looks me in the eye for the first time since he dropped me off after the supply run. 'What do you mean?'

'This. Your apron.' I gesture down at the counter between us. 'It's inhuman.'

He lets out a low chuckle, his exhaustion evident in the slow blink that follows. He must be extremely tired, as it's the only reason he would do what he does in the next few minutes.

First, he walks around the counter to join me behind it with slow, deliberate steps. Then, his arms reach out around my waist to land on the small of my back.

My breath catches.

I feel the tentative caress of his fingers on my back as he tugs at the ribbon holding my apron in its place, his eyes gazing straight into mine. The soft cloth falls away from my waist, and the subtle sensation sends all kinds of naughty clothing-related thoughts firing in all directions inside my brain.

I fight to keep my gaze and my body steady, but I can't help it.

I swallow.

He notices.

This tugs a little at the corner of his lip. 'I can show you if you like.'

The low, almost guttural way the words rumble out of his throat makes me nod yes—frankly, anything he asks might just make me nod yes at this point. Which is why his next words don't elicit a protest from me.

'Turn around.'

I do, and he gently eases his own body against my back, effectively pinning me between his warmth and the counter in front of us. He holds out his arms on either side of me then lays my apron on the countertop. I watch as he demonstrates all the folds and creases, but all my mind can focus on at the moment is the feeling of his arms around me—enveloping my body—touching but not quite.

When he's done, his breath behind my ear makes me shiver. 'Your turn.'

I unravel the cloth with my clammy fingers, but I register nothing, not when he's standing this close. I turn my head to the side so that his face is right over my shoulder, and the longing in my own voice surprises me.

'I think I might need another demonstration.'

The words roll out of my mouth pulsing with . . . something. I don't understand how just a short while alone with Luca has completely ruined me—even the way his breath feels against my nape is pushing me to take action when there's something that I want.

I've always been good at that.

So I lean back against his body just a little bit more and watch as his eyes flicker down from my face to my collarbone to the valley between my breasts.

A shrill alarm slices through the heat in the air and rips Luca away from me.

'Shit.' He grumbles and yanks his phone from his pocket, shutting off the beeping. Everything is doused with the reality of the moment then. Luca curses under his breath before rushing into the back room without another word.

I follow after him, a tidal wave of disappointment washing over me. 'Luca?'

'How do you get home every day?' He rummages through his books on the table without looking at me. 'Do you take the train?'

'Uh, yeah.' I watch him fumble for something imaginary he must've lost somehow. 'It's not so bad.'

'I'll take you home.' He gives up and straightens, a look of defeat in his tired, bloodshot eyes. 'If that's okay?'

'Oh. I don't want to be a bother—'

'You're not.' He ruffles a hand through his hair, somehow looking even more exhausted. 'Please. I . . . want to take you home.'

The memory of our not-so-wholesome position just a while back twists my stomach into naughty little knots. 'Okay.'

'Thank you.' He grabs his keys hanging by the door to the back room. 'Let's go.'

Luca is such a closed book, and I hate that I can never tell exactly what he's thinking. The car ride is pregnant with a weighted silence now, and all my mind keeps flitting back to was the *very* acute sensation he left against my body behind the counter.

Something inside me throbs.

Thankfully, Luca breaks the silence soon after. 'The licensure exam is tomorrow.'

'Shit.' No wonder he's been all over the place today.

'Shit is right.' He stops at an intersection and lets out a long, drawn-out sigh. 'It'll last for two days. You can come to work if you want to or not. Either way . . . ' He reaches inside his pocket and hands me a key.

'Thanks. I'll try not to burn the place down.' I grin at him, but he doesn't return the smile. 'You'll do *fine*, Luca. You've been studying like hell for this.'

'I—' His eyes flicker over to me then he turns a corner. 'The thing is, I'm . . . not sure I'm in the right state of mind to take the exam right now.'

'What do you mean?' I thumb the Tea for Two key before slipping it into my jeans pocket. 'Is something wrong?'

'No. Maybe.' His face morphs into another scowl. He doesn't say anything else.

By the time he pulls up in front of my house, I can tell he still hasn't figured out exactly what he wants to say.

So I make it easier for him. 'Look, whatever it is, don't let it get to you. You've got this.' I shrug. 'And if you need to ease the nerves for a bit, I'm just a message away, okay?'

'Yeah.' He stares at me again. With a slight lip press, he digs his nails into the steering wheel. It's obvious he's holding back whatever's at the tip of his tongue at the moment. 'Yeah. Thanks, Kali.'

'Cool. Thanks for the ride.'

'You're welcome.'

I make a move to get out of the car when he clears his throat. 'Hey, Kali?'   .

'Yeah?'

'Is it okay if I drive you home every night from now on?'

'I really don't mind—'

'It's not safe.' He averts his gaze. 'You know, taking the train this late.'

'Oh.' I bite my lip. 'Um. If you're sure . . . '

'I am.' He locks his eyes onto mine. 'I want to.'

'Okay.'

Finally, he smiles. 'Good night, Kali.'

And that smile instantly renders all my attempts to muzzle my giddiness unsuccessful. I smile back.

'Good night, Luca.'

Radiant

The next two days fly by in a blur. On the first day, I take my shift in the afternoon as always but, for the first time since Uncle Drew appeared in the corner booth, he isn't around. After the initial shock of not seeing him in his usual spot, I spend the next hour theorizing as to what he does when he's away—does he have other things to get to? Some sort of afterlife social gathering, a ghostly mall, a weekend park to wander around outside of haunting hours on the spectral plane?

The existential crisis doesn't last long because the customers start pouring in at around five and don't stop. My petition is somehow doing its job—it's revived a little bit more interest in this place among old patrons who used to hang out here or random strangers who just want to post about it on Instagram.

The second day is just as hectic but Uncle Drew is around again, at least. I ask him where he was the day before and he can't tell me. Apparently, he has no idea he missed a day. All he knows is that he has been at the corner booth, all day, every day—another mystery I'll never be able to explain.

We don't talk about our little non-argument the last time we spoke and that's okay—I guess that's how it is with family. You fight, you make up, you go about your day like nothing happened.

With Frey, though, I haven't had the strength to reach out to her just yet. She knows me well enough not to linger around when I'm mad at her, so it's me who has to take the first step.

I keep telling myself I'm busy—too busy to even send my best friend a simple message.

I'm such a coward.

Speaking of messages, Luca hasn't sent me even one. I mean, it's okay—he's focused on his exam, as he should be. That's all there is to it.

When I show up for my shift on the day Luca's supposed to be back, the CLOSED sign that greets me keeps me rooted to the front step for a good five minutes. The word somehow looks like it's in some kind of foreign script because my mind just can't piece together why the tea shop is still closed. Before he left for the exam, he told me to come in at six tonight, which is why it's even weirder that the shop isn't open.

But then I remember that I have a key, so I don't need to keep picking at my cuticles while gaping at the front door. I slip inside and everything is still just how I left it last night. Nothing has been set up to start entertaining customers, no chairs are in place, no tea leaves brewing behind the counter, no frowning twenty-three-year-old smouldering at himself in the back room. If there's one thing Luca isn't, it's tardy. So, for him to leave Tea for Two like this, something must definitely, definitely be wrong.

Uncle Drew is conveniently absent too, and I'm starting to think he might have another haunt he's busy with apart from me. I'm gonna have to confront him about that the next time he pops by.

I tiptoe up the small spiral stairs to the left corner of the shop and knock on the door that I know leads to his room. 'Luca? Are you in here?'

No answer.

I press my ear against the door, and there's definitely some shuffling inside. He couldn't have been here all night, could he? 'I just want to make sure you're okay.'

A few more seconds of silence later, I fumble for the key in my pocket. Is it possible Luca's given me a master key?

'Look, I'm . . . I'm coming in,' I swallow, shove the key into the lock and turn.

The door opens with a creak.

I step inside. The lights are off, and there, in the middle of the small studio apartment, is the wayward owner of the tea shop in a crumpled heap on the floor.

'Luca!'

I rush to him. 'Luca?'

He groans and rolls over on his back, dropping a limp arm over his forehead. From the looks of his unkempt clothes, he's still in his polo shirt and jeans from last night, the first few buttons of his shirt undone. I try not to get distracted by the chiselled lines disappearing down his neckline and, instead, hold the back of my hand against his neck. There's no fever or anything, but the way his face is all scrunched up makes me wonder if he's actually in some kind of pain.

'Hey. Hey,' I shake his shoulders for a bit, leaning in closer to his face. 'Are you okay?'

He finally opens his eyes at my gentle nudging, and he blinks a few times like he's trying to piece together the mirage that's me, kneeling over him in the darkness of his room like this. 'Kali?'

'What happened?'

'I'm sorry,' he mumbles, his low voice rumbling through the silence of his room. He covers his eyes with his hand again, a tinge of pink staining his cheeks. 'I'm pretty sure I failed the test. I . . . couldn't concentrate on anything.'

My breath catches. Whatever was on his mind must've been what happened right before he left, and the last thing he did was spend all evening with me.

Oh god.

'Luca, I—'

'I'm sorry, Kali,' he mumbles in a fevered haze, his eyes still covered with his palm. 'I kept studying and you kept working and I . . . I should have stayed, I should've helped you . . . '

His voice drifts in and out until he trails right off, and before I can protest his apology, his hand slides down to the floor, unconscious. For a second, I panic that something worse has happened to him, but now that I can see his face clearly, I realize that he's just gone back to sleep. From the looks of it, he hasn't had a single hour of decent rest since he got back, and the exhaustion is evident on his face.

I reach out and graze my fingers over the stray strands of hair on his forehead, his skin glistening with a thin layer of sweat. Whatever he's been obsessing about has obviously kept him up all night. I glance around, tidy up some of the books around him, then try to shift his body to pull him toward his futon on the floor that he missed by barely a few inches.

Luca's dead weight isn't easy to move. When I finally slide him into a comfortable position on his futon, I lay a hand on his forehead again to make sure he's not burning up. The sheen of sweat illuminates his face with an almost otherworldly glow. With nothing else but the moonlight streaming in from his window, Luca looks like a dream.

I make a beeline for his desk, a small table propped up against his window in the corner of the studio. There's nowhere else for me to sit, and while I don't want to leave him like this, I can't join him on his bed, no matter how much I want to make sure he's okay.

In fact, I'm thankful that Luca's desk is facing the window so that I won't have to see his body. I don't trust myself to keep our employer–employee relationship intact, not when he's so, so close.

After a few more minutes of me staring out the window, painfully aware of Luca's sleeping form right behind me, a soft groan makes me whip back around. Luca's face is contorted in pain, and I rush to his side again to lay a hand on his forehead. He seems fine, honestly, but leaning over him like this, my face merely inches away from his, the urge to be close to him takes me by surprise. It's always been there, that yearning, every day when I work behind the counter with him by my side, almost touching in the middle of the cramped space but never getting too close. I've always tried to push it back down, whatever this is, but here, now, with nothing and no one else around, I unravel.

There's only the soft rise and fall of his chest now, the musky scent of his body hurling all my self-control out the window. My stomach churns.

I breathe out to calm my nerves, then I lean closer to give his forehead a quick peck.

He exhales with a soft groan, and the crease on his forehead eases. Now, without the pained frown etched all over his features, he finally looks peaceful.

I close the space between us and brush my lips against his cheek this time. His eyes are still closed, but he shifts.

I freeze.

His lips are right against mine now, and the soft, ever-so-gentle contact electrifies my whole body. Something else replaces the sensation deep in my belly, and I move just a tiny inch closer, pressing my lips against the softness of his. When I withdraw for a fraction of a second, a small whimper escapes his mouth.

I plant another butterfly kiss on his lips, then another, and another. I just can't seem to help myself now, and whatever heat was radiating from his body just a while ago welds the gap between us. When I plant the next kiss with a soft, moist little smack, his lips part ever-so-slightly, and his tongue grazes my lips for a brief second.

My breath catches. My gaze flicks up to his face and his eyes are still closed, but he's brushing his lips against mine again now, and it doesn't take long before he plunges his tongue inside my mouth.

My own eyes flutter close. I moan against his lips just as his own moans start mirroring mine.

I don't even notice how his arm has suddenly wrapped itself around my back, pulling me down over his body with a thud. I press my whole weight against him and a grunt rumbles from his throat. When we part for breath, he whispers, 'Kali . . . '

He claims my mouth again, his breath growing more and more laboured. My fingers frantically start undoing every single button on his shirt, and when I run my hands across his chest, he groans again and slides his hand from the small of my back down to the back of my thigh. He hasn't made any efforts to rid me of my jeans just yet, but with one rough pull, he successfully grinds our hips together and the pressure makes both of us moan even louder at the same time.

My fingers tremble with so much desire. I find myself fumbling with the zipper on his jeans, and when we resurface for air, his eyes finally flutter open.

The moment he sees me there on top of him with both of us in various states of undress, panting and heaving and just so, so hot, I see the steely look in his grey orbs return and, in an instant, the flushed, euphoric look on his face is wiped clean. Instead, total panic takes over as he scurries out from under me, holding both my shoulders away from him at arm's length.

'Shit,' he grumbles, the reality of what we're about to do slicing through the fire in the air. 'Kali, I . . . oh my god, we can't.'

I try to still my own frenzied breathing. 'Luca?'

'I just—you're not—' He inches away from me on his futon and swallows heavily. 'I can't do this with you. I'm sorry.'

He immediately starts redoing his buttons, turning away from me to hide the very prominent bulge straining to break free from his jeans. I frown.

'What do you mean, you can't do this with me?' I grit my teeth, shame and rejection crashing down on me. 'You can't tell me I'm the only one who feels how right this all is—you can't kiss me like that and pretend it doesn't mean anything.'

'It doesn't. I'm not thinking straight, okay?' He turns back to me and stands up from his futon. 'I haven't been thinking clearly since I left.'

'Bullshit.' I rise and glare up at him. 'There's something here, Luca—there always has been. You may be so damn used to hiding your emotions but the way you held me just now—your body can't lie.'

'I—' Luca goes red, but he shakes his head and grits his teeth. 'You're wrong, Kali. I'm just exhausted—I haven't slept properly in days. I can't do this. I'm sorry.'

We stare at each other but while he's trying his best to put up a firm front for me, his eyes betray everything he's denying. And if he's not brave enough to admit his feelings, I shouldn't be stupid enough to try.

I turn around to leave, but Luca's firm hand suddenly gripping my wrist stops me in my tracks. I turn to him and see this weird, almost pained expression on his face, which he holds for a few beats before he finally yanks me toward him.

And kisses me.

His brows are furrowed but my own eyes are wide open in shock and confusion and . . . something else. He ends the kiss with a frown on his face like he's being tortured, like he's still trying to hold himself back.

He lets my hand go.

Somehow, a bizarre summer rainstorm starts up outside like divine intervention, perfectly mirroring the thunderstorm in my heart.

'Kali . . . ' He breathes out, his grey eyes softening. 'I'm sorry. I didn't mean that. I'm just . . . I'm—' He pinches the bridge of his nose and sighs. 'I can't stop thinking about you, and I've been handling everything terribly. I'm not exactly an expert when it comes to . . . whatever this is.' He looks down, and a faint hint of pink flutters across his cheeks. 'I'm sorry and I'm an idiot and if . . . if you want to leave and quit, I totally understand. But I just want you to know that whatever it is you're trying to do with your petition, you can always talk to me about it. If you want to. Or not.'

He raises a hand to his nape. 'I guess I just want to say that I'm here. If you want me to be.'

My heart leaps at the possibility of something that could happen with me and Luca now, but I shake my head. 'Whatever, Luca. I don't need this.'

A quiver of pain sweeps across his features, but he holds it back. 'I'm sorry, Kali. I really am. I shouldn't have toyed with your emotions like this. I'm weak and a huge ass and—' he swallows, 'I really like you, Kali. It took me forever to admit it to myself, but I do. You just . . . you have that life and fire inside you that I could never have, and you're . . . you're radiant.'

He raises his eyes back up at me. 'I can understand if you never want to see me again, and I'll respect that. But if you'll let me, I just want to show you how much you mean to me. Just one shot . . . '

He steps closer, his body now barely an inch away from mine. I hold my ground and stare up at him. He bites his lip with a last bout of hesitation, until he leans down, slowly, carefully, almost like he's asking for my permission, like he's waiting for me to protest. But the tension between us is reverberating through my nerves now, rumbling across my body and heating up the entire room.

He parts his lips and brushes them against mine, soft and scared, the tip of his tongue touching my lips like he's afraid I might burn him. When he finally feels like he's tiptoed around me long enough, he darts his tongue inside my mouth and it immediately makes me whimper against my better judgment. I feel him smile against my lips, and it's all he needs to tilt my chin up higher.

His other hand caresses my hair behind my head, and my eyes finally shut close. I find myself whimpering for the second time, encouraging him to pull me closer. I finally snake my arms up around his neck. He grunts his hunger at me, and we stumble back against his desk with a loud thud.

It's all we need to shake us back to our senses. But even as we part, Luca keeps his hands on my hips. He smiles at me and I smile at him, and even though everything's a mess and the world's a mess and *I'm* a mess, in that tiny space in time, none of it matters.

For a second it's just me and Luca as the thunderstorm rumbles around us, broken hearts and broken dreams forgotten.

Death Blinked into Existence

I fasten the last button on my top and tug at the hem, staring at myself in the mirror—Luca's mirror, to be exact. After a full hour of cuddling on his futon, we both fell into an easy sleep, spooning like a proper couple while the rain outside raged on. By the time I woke up, I found him whipping up some chicken tinola in the kitchen—or what counts as his kitchen given that it's only a single-pot induction cooker propped up on a counter in the corner of the studio.

Retreating to his bathroom gave me an excuse to straighten myself out, and now here I am, gaping at my own reflection like I don't recognize myself, a flush on my face that makes my skin glow. It's the kind of giddiness that swaddles my whole body, seeping into every nook and cranny, illuminating everything and refusing to let go.

I scrunch up my hair and watch it fall down my shoulders with an easy weight. I've always been proud of my just-the-right-amount-of-messy hair—I've been told it's sexy, letting it loose without much maintenance. But the way Luca raked his fingers through my strands every time he kissed me made me messier, wilder, hungrier.

It's not like we got any further than that, though. It was just an hour of making out—a *lot* of making out—and talking about everything under the sun, but it felt like that hour alone already got us all caught up.

A comfortable warmth radiates from inside my chest again, and the girl in the mirror smiles without meaning to.

I am in so much trouble.

'Holy crap.' I curse as soon as I step out of his bathroom. 'That smells *so good*.'

He chuckles, scooping the chicken and soup from the pot into a small bowl. 'Thanks. Broths are the extent of my culinary knowledge, so manage your expectations, please.'

'That's still leaps ahead of me, so consider my expectations managed.' I slink up to him and breathe in the steamy goodness of the dish. 'Perfect for rainy nights, too.'

'All you have to do is chuck everything into boiling water and it's done. Again, the extent of what I know in the kitchen.' He scoops more chicken into another bowl, gives me a peck on the cheek then carries both bowls over to his desk. I follow suit, and he pulls up his chair for me. He leans against the wall beside the desk, tilting his head.

'What?'

He smiles at me then—in fact, he hasn't stopped smiling since our little . . . thing. I like the way he smiles.

I like it a lot.

'Nothing.' He licks his lips. 'You look beautiful.'

I grin. 'You're just saying that because I let you make out with me.'

He chuckles again, his eyes crinkling. 'And I will forever be honoured.' He picks up a bowl and nods at the other one on the desk. 'Dig in.'

'Thanks.' I close my eyes and take a deep breath, letting the aroma of the chicken tinola make a statement inside my brain. 'I do feel a little worried that you're standing there with a piping hot bowl of soup in your hands.'

'Sorry. My studio's furniture has a single-person occupancy limit.'

We enjoy our broth in silence for a while, the pitter-patter of the rain outside slowing down to a light drizzle. Every so often, I look up and catch Luca gazing down at me, and he smiles each time I do. I guess he can't keep the giddiness down either, and I can't blame him—I know exactly how he feels, and I don't think I want this afterglow to end.

Two empty bowls later, we're back on the futon, him still in his jeans with the first few buttons on his top provocatively undone. I trace a finger along his collarbone and frown. 'This can't be right.'

He props his head up with his hand and turns to his side to face me. 'What do you mean?'

'This.' I let my finger trail down to his chest. 'You don't look like the type who works out, and yet look at this. It's not fair.'

'I jog every other morning.'

'That shouldn't translate to *this*.' I poke at a carefully toned bicep. 'I blame it on good genes, which is a cop-out.'

He grins. 'You're one to talk—with your yoga and this whole milk tea-tasting philosophy you bring with you. You have no right being that sexy when you walked into the shop that day.'

'I . . .' I trail off. 'You thought I was sexy?'

'Hell yes,' he mumbles then leans in close for a full-on kiss. Luca tangles his fingers in my hair again and tugs my face even closer, and I whimper against his mouth. He sneaks another quick peck in after we part then leans back down on his back with a hand behind his head. I lower myself on top of his chest, and my Cheetos pendant dangles down my neck.

He eyes the tacky little thing swaying back and forth in front of his face. 'Big Cheetos fan?'

The question should be harmless, but it clutches at the frayed edges of my heart, and Luca senses my hesitation. The playful smile on his lips fades. 'Kali?'

I'm somewhere else now. The rain and the chicken tinola and the warmth of Luca's skin all disappear from reach, and all that's left now is the blood of my favourite person in the whole wide world smeared on the pavement between after-school rendezvouses and guild battles on my phone. There's a tattered newsboy cap flung to one side, a look of permanent shock plastered on what should've been a smiling face, my Cheetos pendant the only thing that I can hold onto, the only piece of Uncle Drew that I have left.

A single tear trickles down my cheek and scalds my skin.

Luca wraps his arms around me then, and all of a sudden it's out there, here, now, all the pain and the memories and the injustice of it all, and I sob into his chest because there's no room for the old me anymore, the carefree Kali who could dream big and aim high and see her future ahead of her, all smiles and cheers and passing praises. There's no room for the future now, not when all I want is to stay with the ghost of my uncle forever.

I always thought that Death owes me for Uncle Drew, but maybe it's not enough—maybe Death wants more, wants my happiness, wants all of me to remember that I don't deserve moments like these.

Death blinked into existence when Uncle Drew left. It's never going to leave me now, and I'm never going to let it.

I look up at Luca's face and let the pain in. 'There's something you should know.'

* * *

Luca grips my hand the next morning, and the two of us pause at the entrance to Jollibee. It's not just *any* Jollibee though—it's *the* Jollibee, the one where Luca's supposed to be helping me score multiple signatures for my petition.

It's also *the* Jollibee of Luca's super private, super exclusive LEGO group—something I never thought he'd be into, not with the super serious way he's been burying his nose into his books. But then again, there's that stud on his left ear, which I'm sure comes with a pretty interesting backstory—but I guess that's a revelation for another day.

Right now, I'm still reeling from the tiny revelation that Luca isn't at all what I initially pegged him to be . . . and I like it.

He throws me a sideways smile. 'You ready?'

I bite my lip. 'Are *you*?'

He glances at the Jollibee and then back at me, crinkling his nose. 'I'm not, to be honest. They'll descend on you like vultures on prey.'

'I can handle it,' I shrug. 'It just means they care about you that much.'

'That, and that I've never brought a girl with me to any of our meets before.'

Given how expertly Luca took my breath away last night, I doubt he's a newbie to the relationship department. But if I'm the only one who's privileged enough to share this side of him, I'll gladly take it.

I squeeze his hand back. 'I'm the queen of small talk, remember? Don't worry—I'll charm the pants off them.'

His eyes travel down to my lips for a beat. 'No out-charming pants, please. All activities related to undressing should be reserved just for me.'

My stomach writhes. 'Yes, sir.'

We step inside the fast food chain and weave through the lines snaking in front of the counter. The function room sits quietly at the back of the store, and the moment we reach the door, the girl sitting on the makeshift reception desk shoots up from her seat.

'Oh my god—you're Kali.' She pierces me with her black gaze, her face devoid of any emotion, in stark contrast with the streaks of electric blue in her hair. She stretches her arms in front of her and deadpans, 'Give me a hug.'

'Um. Okay. Hi.' I fall into her arms in an awkward pose and she immediately crushes me into her tiny frame. Luca's a full head taller than me, so I'm not the most noticeable kid in the bunch. But this spunky-but-not-quite girl is even shorter—although that doesn't mean she can't give a mean hug.

She wags a finger at Luca beside me when we part then turns her dark gaze back to me. 'Do *not* let this boy break your heart. And if he does, I'll have you know that I'm vengeance incarnate, and I will personally break into his secret LEGO stash and crush every single one of his bricks until they're nothing but sand.'

I bite back a grin. 'Duly noted.' I glance up at Luca, who's actually rolling his eyes. 'You have a secret LEGO stash?'

'I'll show you when we get back.' Luca waves his hand at me then sighs. 'Lee, just sign us in.'

'Right.' The girl slumps back in her seat and scribbles our names in her logbook. Luca pays our entrance fee, and she presents us with two paper wristbands in return.

'I'm Lee, by the way, and I run this ship,' she says when she hands me my wristband, her gaze intensifying. 'I am the mother of all my LEGO-loving children. He puts a single toe out of line, you come to me, non-LEGO-related shenanigans included.'

'Cool. I will.' I flash her a grin while Luca rolls his eyes again, grabbing my hand to drag me past her. She doesn't let her gaze drop until we're through.

I like Lee.

I barely get the chance to ask Luca more about her when the function room comes alive in front of me, promptly shoving my brain into sensory overload. Lined up against all four walls are tables filled to the brim with LEGO sets of all shapes and sizes, most of them still in mint-condition boxes as the people behind the tables sell their wares. In the middle of the room are even more stalls cramped together with polybags and loose parts, bricks meticulously categorized into plastic boxes and grid containers, organizers arranged into colours and sizes and studs and minifigs. Some of the tables have actual built displays of everything from Marvel sets to architectural landmarks—bursts of colour and life and laughter, clicking and chatting and celebrating this beautiful, shared passion.

The din of the chatter adds to the buzzing in the room, but when Luca steps in, most of the people behind the tables turn to look at him.

And the cheering begins.

'Luca!' A group of men and women to our left waves us over, and Luca's often-stoic face bursts into a genuine smile. My heart is *not* ready for this.

They all swap greetings and high-fives and everyone immediately turns to me, showering me with too much love and attention—I don't think I've ever felt like this since my top-of-the-pyramid days.

'You must be Kali!'

'Welcome to our humble home away from home.'

'What's your favourite LEGO set?'

'How did you get this guy to finally introduce someone to us?'

'Come take a seat right here!'

'How did you two meet?'

I'm overwhelmed by the slew of questions left and right, and it almost feels like I've just been thrust into a family reunion with the way everyone's genuinely interested in me and . . . whatever my situation with Luca is. I realize I don't know what Luca told his friends when he told them about me, except that, apparently, he was bringing me with him today. How did he introduce me, exactly? What am I to him now? And what is he to me?

Despite all the questions closing in on me and Luca trying to catch up with old friends at the same time, he doesn't let my hand go. Not even for a second.

What began as a simple Facebook group with a handful of friends who loved LEGO apparently grew into this thing that it is today, and they hold these meet-ups every month in different places, selling merch and sets and catching up with everyone's lives at the same time. It feels surreal to be surrounded by this much life again, this tiny community of love and mutual support, all born from a humble little brick.

As soon as the interrogation is over, Luca tells them all about my petition, conveniently leaving out the parts about Uncle Drew. Every single person in the room offers me their signature wholeheartedly, and by the time the afternoon ends—with a tour of every booth and Luca explaining all the sets to me in gruesome detail—my petition leaves the function room sixty signatures fuller.

'Here.' Lee types in her number on my phone when we pass by her table to leave. 'Text me. I got you, girl.'

'Thanks, Lee,' I stretch out my arms to her this time, and she gladly reciprocates—still with the deathly look in her black, black eyes and that tone that does make her sound like Vengeance Incarnate. Luca shakes his head beside us, but I catch a small smile dancing across his lips for the briefest second.

I turn to him with a smirk the moment we get into his car. 'I have *so many questions.*'

'I brought this upon myself.' He pulls away from the kerb and chuckles. 'Fire away.'

'Okay, first of all, can you show me all your LEGO sets?'

'They're unbuilt, mind you. I haven't had the time or the space to piece them together,' he says. 'And yes, Kali, I already told you I would.'

'Good.' I peek into the paper bag on my lap at our mini-haul—one LEGO set of a bubble tea shop and another of a mobile coffee cart. 'Second, did you tell them I was your girlfriend?'

Luca doesn't reply, and just like that, all the euphoria of the event crumbles down. There's a different kind of churning in my stomach now, and it makes my rose-coloured glasses fade to crystal.

Crisp. Clear. No-nonsense.

Real.

We don't say anything else after that. I keep my eyes trained on my Chucks, and I don't even realize that Luca has already stopped driving.

I look up. We're parked at the neighbourhood circle, a stretch of stone benches littered on the sidewalk amid outdoor diners and cafes. The place is usually packed with employees letting off steam at night, but in the middle of the afternoon with the sun setting over the horizon like this, the uncertainty lingers. The darkness hasn't settled in just yet, leaving a tentative buzzing in the air. The bar-hopping scene hasn't started—not quite empty but not quite alive, it mirrors the palpable hesitation between us.

'Let's talk for a bit,' Luca turns to me, his voice softening. 'Is that okay?'

I nod and we both get out of the car. He takes my hand in his again and we stroll down to the nearest bench, Luca stretching his arm around the back like he did when we were inside his campus. This time though, he pulls my body against his, and I find the crook of his arm a perfect fit.

It seems so long ago now, that day on campus when all I could do was obsess over nestling my body against the tiny space between us. It's only been a short while, to be honest, but why does it feel like everything's changed but nothing's changed? I'm still adamant on saving the cafe, still stubborn enough to refuse to let Uncle Drew go. Telling Luca all about it hasn't changed anything—no matter what's happened between us overnight.

And that alone is already breaking my heart.

'I've decided to head back home.' Luca breaks the silence first, but what he says makes it much, much worse. 'The results will be out tomorrow, but I already know I won't be on the list.'

'I'm so sorry, Luca.'

He shakes his head. 'Don't be. I liked thinking about you. It drove me crazy, but I liked it.' He plants a kiss on my head. 'But the more I think about it, the more I realize that failing the exam is probably the best thing that's ever happened to me—except you, of course.'

I tilt my head up at him beside me. 'What do you mean?'

'It's like you said. I should learn to smell the roses and taste the tea and all that. Maybe failing is just what I need. Maybe it's telling me to slow down, to rethink my priorities, to figure out where to go from here. Maybe it's telling me to go home.' A sad smile mutes the colours on his face. 'I'd ask you to stay with me, despite being islands apart. But I already know where your heart is, and I can't ask you to change that for me.'

He sighs. 'So, to answer your earlier question, no, I didn't tell them you were my girlfriend. I wasn't sure you wanted me to.' A quiver of hesitation sweeps across his face. 'Do you . . . want me to?'

I don't think I'm prepared for this kind of question this early in our non-existent relationship, but that's Luca—always moving down his to-do list, always efficient, always eager to get things over with. I guess I'm grateful he's not one to beat around the bush—there's no skirting around with him, and if we're going to end before we even begin, there's no better way than this.

'I want you to . . . ' I look away. 'But I don't think you should.'

He sighs and doesn't say anything else. We stay cuddled that way for a while, his hand tightening around my shoulder, almost like he's afraid I'll disappear if he let go. I fight hard to keep the euphoria from last night enveloped around us, but there's something else in here with us now, chalking itself into the fragile walls of my little bubble and threatening to make it burst.

Something hard and heavy lodges itself in my throat, and I shove it back down. I look up at him. 'So what now?'

Another sad smile sneaks its way onto Luca's lips. 'That's up to you. I'll take what I can get.'

A couple strolls past us, hand in hand and in love, and I wish we could be just like them, oblivious to the cracks on the surface and the thunderstorm raging underneath. Starting anything with Luca would only mean I owe Time a favour, at the mercy of its cruel sands slipping from my fingers, despite clawing at it in a desperate attempt to hold on. But I'd rather spend this time with him than let him slip away—I made that mistake with Uncle Drew, and I'm not going to make the same mistake again.

'Before you go.' I clasp my hand over his and intertwine our fingers. 'Just because it's not going to last doesn't mean we shouldn't be together now. Let's just enjoy what we have before you go.'

'I figured.' He squeezes my hand back and runs his thumb across my skin. 'Before I go.'

As I lay my head on his shoulder and he breathes in the scent of my hair, his last three words hover around us like a promise, teetering on the edge of heartbreak.

Will He Remember Me Then?

I shift from one foot to another in front of the door to Freyja's condo unit, like I've been doing for a good fifteen minutes now. Fighting with her always leaves me with this vibrating pit at the bottom of my stomach, an urge to throw up and poop at the same time. It's not pretty.

Taking a deep breath, I reach out to ring the doorbell when the door to the unit swings open. The whirlwind that is my best friend strides out of the doorway and almost slams into my awkward frame.

'Kali!' Her eyes widen. The jumbo bag of Cheetos in her hand slips to the floor with a hefty crunch that echoes down the hallway. She picks it up in one swift motion and shoves it into my arms.

'I'm sorry,' we both blurt out at the same time.

She shakes her head. 'You have nothing to be sorry for. I, on the other hand, was the jerk who said all those things and waited forever before apologizing about it.' She crinkles her nose. 'Wait a minute. What were you doing standing here?'

'I was going to apologize.'

'Well, I was going to do it first. I was heading out to Tea for Two before you ruined my surprise.'

'I beat you to it, then,' I grin and hold up the Cheetos bag. 'Peace offering?'

'Peace offering.' She grins back. 'Since you're here anyway, wanna hang out?'

'Sure.'

'Fab.' Frey grabs my arm and tugs me inside. As she leads me to her room, past the living area, her mom pops her head out of the kitchen and catches me mid-pull. We stop short.

'Kali!' She straightens her ponytail and beams at me, the spark in her eyes mirroring Freyja's perfectly. 'So lovely to see you again.'

'Hi Mrs Reyes,' I return the smile as she approaches. 'Sorry to barge in unannounced.'

'Nonsense! You can barge in any time you want.' She tilts her head at me, the way all adults do when they're trying their best to sympathize. 'And how are you doing since . . . since school ended?'

I doubt Mrs Reyes is interested in my last day at school because, looking at the way her eyes are softening at me with that maternal look I know so well, I'm pretty sure I know what she's talking about. Everyone who heard about Uncle Drew has been tiptoeing around me, like a head tilt and a small how-are-you will make the grief go away.

She means well, though—they all do. But no amount of sympathetic smiles and softened tones can bring Uncle Drew back.

'I'm doing great,' I lie. 'College is pretty exciting.'

Mrs Reyes's face lights up, probably relieved that she doesn't have to linger on the grief hanging over my head.

'It is, isn't it? Freyja here is already gearing up for a handful of choices.'

I feel my best friend stiffen beside me, telling me she hasn't exactly revealed her plans to her folks just yet.

'And Ryan's already set for law school. Isn't he, hon?' Mrs Reyes turns to Frey, who smiles through gritted teeth.

'Yep,' she says. 'All set.'

'How about you, Kali?' Mrs Reyes turns her attention back to me. 'Are you seeing anyone lately?'

'Okay, we gotta go, Ma!' Frey clutches my arm and yanks me into her room, and I throw her mom one last sheepish smile before Frey shuts the door.

'Sorry,' she mumbles the moment we're safely inside and away from prying mothers and their well-meaning questions. 'Saved your ass, though, didn't I? Would've been an awkward conversation.'

The memory of Luca's lips against mine sears into my mind at that exact moment. Something tingles inside me.

'Yeah . . . about that.'

'"*About that?*"' Freyja's jaw drops, and her face bursts into a colour palette I have only ever seen when she plays her music. 'Holy crap. There's *someone*.'

'Well—'

'It's Luca.' She flat-out just says it like it's a given—it's not even a question. I'm apparently a transparent mess.

I can't help but smile then, the giddiness coming back to me in waves. I nod.

'You wily fox.' She sits me on the bed across her and tucks her legs under her. 'Tell. Me. Everything.'

'Before you get too excited, there's a caveat.'

'A *caveat*?' She shakes her head. 'You've been spending way too much time with Ryan.'

'But there is,' I say. 'Luca and I aren't a thing. He's flying back home to Cebu, and we're not going to do the Long Distance Relationship thing. We're just . . . enjoying each other's company right now. I don't even know what we are.'

'Oh my god—he's an idiot.' Frey folds her arms across her chest. 'There's no easier time than now to do the LDR thing! Hasn't he heard of this technological advancement called *the internet*?'

'Well . . . ' I avert my gaze and fixate on the U2 poster pinned on the wall behind Freyja. 'It was actually my idea.'

'Then you're *both* idiots.' She groans. 'Enlighten me, please.'

'We're having fun *now*. It doesn't have to be forever. If he leaves then he leaves.'

'If you're trying to sound cool by being all casual about this, it's not working.'

'I mean it, Frey. I can't afford any distractions. It can't get farther than this.'

Freyja clutches at her hair and groans. 'Kali, *please*. I know your laser focus is on Uncle Drew, and I respect that. I do. I just don't think pushing away the possibility of—dare I say it—*love* is going to help with your future.'

'I can't care about my future at the moment. You already know that.' I grit my teeth. 'Are we going to have the same stupid fight again?'

'No, Kali. I just feel like you should think this through more.'

'I will when I'm done with my petition. Luca helped me get sixty more signatures in a day, by the way. He also offered to introduce me to the landlord to present my petition.'

'So you told him all about Uncle Drew?'

'Yes.'

'And he didn't judge you for it?'

'No.'

'And he's helping you with the petition?'

'Yes.'

'Kali.'

The sympathetic head tilt comes from Freyja this time, but it's a look that tells me she knows I'm doing something stupid, and the tragic thing about it is that I'm actually aware of it.

She sighs then. 'Look, I'll help you with your petition, too, okay? I've still got your back. I'm doing a live stream tomorrow. We'll get more signatures then.'

'Thanks, Frey.' I sigh too, rubbing my fingers against my temples. 'And I hear you, okay? I do. I'm not that dense. I just . . . I just need to focus on the petition before anything else. Uncle Drew hasn't been popping into the shop lately and, every day, I worry he's not going to come back. And if that happens, I—'

An oppressive lump rises in my throat, and the grief threatens to consume me again. I shake it off, but Frey catches the slight tremble in my voice. 'If that happens,' I whisper, 'I don't think I'll be strong enough to bear it.'

I let my gaze wander to safer, more neutral territory, afraid that if I look into my best friend's eyes and she sees the scars inside, I might just shatter into a million pieces. My eyes roam over the organized clutter on Freyja's desk—her laptop propped up nicely on a stand, her neon pink headphones hanging on the pegboard on the wall in front of the desk, littered with charging cables, a calendar, rainbow-coloured scrunchies, and a photo of me, her, and Ryan stuffing our faces with unli-pizza at last year's World Pizza Day. There's a boom arm clamped to the edge of her desk with a mic hanging from its tip, and her sticker-filled guitar is nestled on her computer chair right in front of it.

This small snapshot of Freyja's room alone already screams a pretty loud and vibrant picture of her life, and it breaks my heart not to have the same thing.

Maybe all I have is Uncle Drew now, the one thing that makes sense in the present, and maybe I don't want that to change. Maybe piecing together a patch of Freyja and a patch of Ryan and a patch of Luca into my life isn't going to make it whole, not as whole as it was before that dreaded day.

Maybe I'm just struggling to clutch at my own frayed edges now, and one wrong tug will send me spooling out of control, the threads that hold me together unravelling until there's nothing left.

'I love you, Kal,' Freyja says, offering her silence when everything suddenly seems too loud.

'I love you, Frey,' I reel in the sadness with a smile. 'Are we digging into the Cheetos or not?'

* * *

'Uncle Drew, Luca. Luca, Uncle Drew.'

Luca flashes a genuine smile, sitting across Uncle Drew in the corner booth the next day, making sure to close Tea for Two for a bit while we made the introductions. I expect him to act all awkward in front of my uncle—who decided to grace us with his presence today—but all he does is turn up the Luca charm like he's genuinely pleased.

'Nice to finally meet you, sir.'

'I knew it.' Uncle Drew smirks at me in front of us, then returns Luca's smile. 'He can be pretty charming without that frown he's hiding behind all the time.'

'Uncle Drew says you're charming,' I say to Luca, 'and he's being pretty cocky about it.'

Luca chuckles. 'Sorry. I kept trying to steel myself from you, but I guess I've been pretty obvious this whole time.'

'Ah,' Uncle Drew's eyes widen at me. 'I was talking about *your* transparent feelings, but there you go.'

I roll my eyes, and Luca shifts his gaze from me to the space in front of us. 'What did he say?'

'Nothing,' I grin as Uncle Drew adjusts his newsboy cap with a smug look on his face. 'He's just being a wise-ass, which is ironic given how he's never had a long-term relationship himself.'

'Hey!'

I giggle at Uncle Drew's expense, and Luca smiles at me. 'He's happy for us, though. I know he is.'

'I am.' Uncle Drew finally gives us a genuine smile. 'I like seeing you like this. There's a glow in your eyes, Kali. Not that there wasn't one before, but this one's different. Like you're hopeful, happy. Like you're finally moving on.'

I look down then, Uncle Drew's words twisting a knife in my side. Luca peers down at my face, but I whip out my phone before he says anything.

'We've got more signatures now, Uncle Drew. Freyja's live stream just added forty more.' I show him my phone's screen, and Uncle Drew gives me a layered smile laced with something I can't quite place.

'How does Freyja's live stream work?' He leans forward and squints at my screen. 'Do people need to pay or something?'

'Nothing as complicated as that.' I shrug. 'She goes live on YouTube and plays songs for an hour or so, hoping to raise awareness about the petition and gain enough signatures from her followers and supporters.'

'That's pretty cool. Please thank her for me.' Then, Uncle Drew turns to Luca, who's been sitting there quietly while my uncle and I have a conversation he can't hear. 'So Kali. Since you're introducing your boyfriend to me—'

'He's not my—'

'—it only makes sense that I grill him like in a proper interrogation.' Uncle Drew grins. 'Does he have what it takes?'

I nudge Luca beside me. 'My uncle is asking if he can interrogate you.'

'Oh.' Luca looks confused for a bit, but he quickly recovers. 'Yeah, sure. I'm an open book.'

'We'll see about that.' Uncle Drew straightens his cuffs as part of his so-called intimidation technique, but I roll my eyes and hold back a giggle. 'First question. What are your intentions toward my little Kali Shandy?'

I relay the question to Luca, conveniently leaving out my uncle's silly pet name for me. It was apparently based on this super old, carbonated drink or something during his time, but I'll never understand it.

Luca looks visibly flustered, which just proves how seriously he's taking all this when he can't even see his interrogator. 'We're . . . we're keeping things casual for now, sir, because it's what Kali wants, and I respect her for it. Whether things move forward from here or not is up to her, and she has every freedom to decide what she wants.'

'Huh. Good answer, but I'll have to ask *you* about that later.' Uncle Drew narrows his eyes at me. 'You're next, young lady.'

'It's Luca you're here to grill, not me.' I scrunch up my nose at him. 'Next question.'

'You're not getting off the hook,' Uncle Drew says, then turns to Luca again. 'Family background?'

'My parents run a cafe in Cebu City,' Luca replies after I relay the question. 'My father had a stroke five years ago, and life stopped for him—for all of us. He's okay now, but those few weeks before his full recovery felt excruciatingly slow, like everything had gelled into a bullet of time and there was nothing any of us could do.' He surveys his hands for a bit then stares at the empty space in front of us again. 'I swore I wouldn't let life slow down the same way again, so I made a promise to myself to keep moving.'

'Wow. Okay,' Uncle Drew softens his gaze at Luca, who's now fixating on a coffee stain on the table. 'That went downhill pretty fast. I'm sorry about that.'

'Uncle Drew says he's sorry,' I tell Luca, who shakes his head.

'It's all good. Kali gave me the wake-up call I needed, that it's okay to slow down too, for the things that matter.' Luca turns to me then. 'The results came out this morning, by the way. I didn't make it.'

'Luca . . . ' I hold my hand over his on the table, and he doesn't pull away. We spend a few seconds staring at each other, and while I know Uncle Drew doesn't know what's happening, he mercifully offers us his silence.

'It's okay, really,' Luca whispers to me, trying to convince me with a small smile. 'I'm okay. Next question, please.'

Uncle Drew clears his throat. 'Okay, well . . . future plans?'

'I'm going home. I'm going to spend time with my parents while I can, and maybe it'll make more sense than trying to keep moving all the time. Maybe I should've been spending more time with them after my father's stroke instead of moving farther and farther away.' Luca answers Uncle Drew's relayed question without taking his eyes off me, almost like he's pleading. For a second I forget we're inside Tea for Two, but the ghostly spectre in my periphery lingers, reminding me of everything I don't want to let go.

'But, until then, before I go,' Luca goes on, 'I'll be right here, with Kali, before I go.'

Luca doesn't say anything else then, and neither does Uncle Drew. I have to fight to break eye contact, because I don't think I can handle the look in Luca's eyes right now.

I nod at Uncle Drew. 'Any more questions?'

He shakes his head. 'Not for him.'

'Right. We should get back to work.' I scoot over and stand up, averting my eyes from the confused, judgemental, and sympathetic look I know Uncle Drew's shooting me right now. Luca hesitates for a bit before sliding out of the booth too, but not before smiling in Uncle Drew's general direction.

'Great talking to you, sir.'

Luca sneaks a quick peck on my cheek and heads into the back room like a mirage, leaving me with a ghost of my own. Uncle Drew sighs.

'Kali. Can we talk for a bit?'

'Sure,' I stare straight into his translucent face. 'Is it about the guild? Summer vacation? College courses? My job? The petition?'

Uncle Drew hesitates. 'No, but—'

'Then I can't. I have to get back to work.'

A shudder of pain flits across Uncle Drew's face for a split second, ruining this pristine image I have of him, of his perpetual smile and eternal cheekiness, the expression on his face that never falters, never takes anything seriously. The shudder latches onto my mind's eye and clutches on for dear life.

'Sorry, Uncle Drew.' I steel myself, because no matter how much I do want to talk to him and spend more time with him and keep him speaking with me and laughing with me and hanging out in my life forever, I don't want him to question my choices when it comes to this thing with Luca, not with the way Freyja made it clear I'm making the wrong decision.

An annoying little twitch squeezes my chest and something fast and hot almost slips through my defences and onto my eyes, but I swallow hard and shove it all down.

Uncle Drew smiles at me like it's no big deal. 'Sure, kiddo. I'll be right here. Always.'

That last word makes that little squeeze in my chest claw at my heart even harder because he's *not* always here, not recently. He hasn't been popping up as frequently as I hoped he would, and the worst part is that he doesn't even know it, isn't even aware that he's already slipping away, one excruciating day at a time.

I grit my teeth and turn away, but I barely make it a few steps before I whip my head back around just to check if he's still there, just to see if Death hasn't snatched him away unceremoniously, like it did that day on the kerb. But he is, he is, and Uncle Drew's still there, sitting in the booth like nothing happened, like me stepping away for one second didn't make the panic sink its claws into my skin and drag me down. He's still smiling at me like he thinks everything is going to be okay, but it's not, because tomorrow he might not be here, and he's not even going to know it.

Then, I'll still be that little six-year-old kid replaying that Lumpy Space Princess video on loop over and over again, and he'll still be the same uncle with a tolerant smile on his tired face, still willing to spend every waking hour with me just to keep me entertained despite his exhaustion. He'll always be that for me and there won't be any new memories left, because he doesn't even know he's gone. Will he remember me then?

When he moves on where he needs to go, will he even look back and reminisce about this stubborn girl who tried so desperately to cling to him with every ounce of energy she had, or will he just disappear, and I'll never get to say goodbye, just like I didn't get to that day?

The last thought descends on me and adds to the weighted veil around me, but because I'm a fool and a coward and I've learned nothing, I keep walking.

The Void He Left in His Wake

Dear Kali,

Happy eighteenth birthday! Okay, okay, so writing letters isn't cool, but it's your eighteenth, and you didn't get a fancy party or anything, so I figured I should try to make it special by sending you this legit, handwritten letter. Who needs a party anyway, right?

So, I'm not an expert on this kind of thing but let me give it a shot. I've watched you grow from a teeny tiny little thing to this lovely and elegant lady who kicks ass as an Aswang Commander and loves trolling me with memes. I know you think you've only got me without your parents around, but it's me who's trying so desperately to cling onto you, you know? I have no one, and I guess that's kinda sad. My job's fun, but at the end of the day, video games can only do so much, right? And it's only fun when you have someone to play with.

I guess my point is that I'm honoured to be your pal because it's like you chose me for some reason, even

111

though I'm not worthy. You make my life brighter and better, and I want you to know that I'll happily spend the rest of my life making sure you're happy too, whatever that means and whatever it takes.

And I don't mean that slime you broke up with last year. We'll find you a better one—someone who knows your worth and who'll put you first because you deserve to be first. Someone who will celebrate the life and fire inside you and strive to be a better man for you. Someone who's head over heels in love with you for all your beauty and your scars, who respects you and your decisions because you're your own woman, and no one can hold you down. Let's make that my life goal, all right? I won't rest until I know you've found The One. He's out there, kiddo. Seriously. And I'll only be happy if you're happy. No buts.

Okay, so I know I said you don't need a party, but I did say I want you to be happy, so let's throw one at my condo. Invite your friends and we'll paint the town red. See how cool I am now?

Don't forget to bring Cheetos.

Love always,
Your Fire_Drewid

Ryan straightens his tie beside me then reaches over to brush imaginary lint off my shoulder. I've been telling him to stop fidgeting, but he can't help it—Ryan is Ryan, and he will always exude his Ryan-ness everywhere he goes.

Which is what makes him endearing, to be honest. He is the same straight arrow he's always been since he bumped into Frey and me during snack time on the first day of kindergarten. Then, he promptly offered to let us cut in line in front of him to grab the apple juice box on the table, launching into a spiel about women's rights along the way.

'Be cool,' I shush him. 'She's not going to magically appear out of thin air.'

'You don't know the principal as well as I do,' Ryan retorts, pushing his glasses up his nose. 'She hates tardiness, and I, for one, am not going to be on her bad side.'

'School's over, Ry. What are you even trying to be in her good graces for?'

'People in the academe talk.' He gestures around us at the waiting room we've been holed up in for a good half hour now. Summer classes are still in full swing, so it's not like the principal's office is closed or anything. But Principal Siy is a busy woman, so this audience with her is something only Ryan can pull off.

So, I guess I can understand his obsession about making sure he's got a good reputation when these academe peeps 'talk'. Case in point: we're here right now precisely because we're trying to get Principal Siy to help us raise enough signatures for my petition. Ryan already wrote her an email about it—a perfectly crafted, perfectly Ryan email, no doubt—but we still want to show up personally just to prove we're serious about it. If it weren't for him, though, I probably would never have this chance.

Just as Ryan starts fidgeting with his tie again—something he didn't even have to wear, honestly—the door bursts open and a middle-aged woman in a navy jumpsuit smiles at us.

'Ryan, Kali. Come on in.' Principal Siy straightens the high ponytail on her head and motions for us to step inside. Ryan doesn't need to be told twice—he shoots up from our seat and marches into the principal's office like he's in trouble. I follow suit.

I've never gotten into enough trouble to get summoned here throughout my high school life, but it still feels a little awkward, sitting in front of the principal's desk like we're being interrogated.

'So, you're here about Tea for Two, yes?' Principal Siy folds her hands in front of her when we settle down in our seats. 'I read your email, Mr Francisco. You make quite a compelling case.'

'Thank you, ma'am.' Ryan straightens up in his seat, like he can sit any more properly than he already is. 'I hope I've gotten your attention.'

'You have, and frankly, you both didn't have to come in today. I can endorse this to the faculty and they can try and bring it up during their summer classes.' Principal Siy smiles at us both then turns to me. 'I'm just a little curious about why you're interested in saving the place. Any particular relationship with the owners?'

Ryan nudges me, and I clear my throat. 'Not in particular, Principal Siy. We just . . . we just want to keep it as it is. People have made lots of memories there.'

'Ah. It used to be a dim sum place, you know? Back in my day. It's nice that you're thinking about the next batch of students even after you leave.' She doesn't take her eyes off me. 'Speaking of leaving, Ms Ang, have you decided on which university you'd like to attend? I know Mr Francisco here is set on Ateneo.'

The odd scratching in the back of my throat starts up again, but I swallow. 'Not yet, ma'am, but I'm working on it.'

'I'm sure you are.' She leans back in her chair. 'You certainly brightened up our school events while you were here, Ms Ang. Any university would be lucky to have you.'

'Thank you, Principal Siy. That's nice of you to say.'

She smiles at us again, then takes a deep breath. 'Well! Are we done here?'

'Of course, ma'am. Thank you, ma'am.' Ryan leaps from his seat again and nods his head, like he hasn't been here with the principal a hundred times before. 'Thank you so much!'

'Thank you, Principal Siy,' I say, and we both make a beeline for the door. The moment we're out of earshot, it's my turn to elbow Ryan beside me. 'You're such a dweeb,' I grin at him. 'You were acting like we were in the presence of royalty back there.'

'Sorry,' he lets out a huge sigh. 'We got what we wanted though, right?'

'We did, and I will forever be grateful to you.' I wrap my arms around his skinny frame in a massive hug and he snickers. 'Unlimited milk tea on me all month.'

'You're only offering because you know I don't like milk tea.' He scrunches his nose. 'I won't say no to pizza, though.'

'Fine—unlimited pizza on me for a whole day,' I say. 'They'd better have a good pizza joint in Ateneo or they might just feel the dreaded Wrath of Pizza-deprived Ryan Francisco, patent pending.'

'They should, and you will too if you don't start talking right now. That's right—Frey and I talk, in case you don't know.' Ryan smirks at me then with a boyish grin, making him look out of place in his tie and too-stiff polo shirt. He and Freyja look just about as opposite as opposites go, from Frey's weekly wardrobe change to Ry's same-coloured shirt that he wears every day like he's trying to be Mark Zuckerberg.

'Before you grill me about whatever it is you want me to *talk* about, let me tell you this—stop being such an ass.'

He blinks. 'Excuse me?'

'Frey. She told me you were being an ass, and I assume it's because you told her to pursue her dreams and forget about Ateneo?'

'Well, yeah, but—'

'I agree with you, Ry. But you don't have to be such a jerk about it, you know? You don't have to be such a straightforward and practical person all the time. Maybe a little bit more empathy?'

He frowns, but instead of launching into a perfectly worded spiel about the pros and cons of college decisions, he stays silent.

'Yeah,' he whispers after a while. 'Yeah. You're right.'

'Good.'

He clears his throat then. 'Now that that's done, it's my turn to go all judgey on you. So, tell me, Kali,' he smirks. 'What's *really* the deal between you and Luca?'

* * *

'Ryan was asking about you yesterday.'

'Yeah?' Luca angles his knife. 'We should probably have dinner together or something. Just the four of us.' He slits a quick incision on his *ampalaya* just as the instructor claps his hands up front.

'You should all be soaking your bitter gourds in saltwater by now, which you'll need to do for twenty minutes or more,' the chef barks out to the room, and my eyes scan all the students at the cooking stations in front of us. There's a reason Luca and I picked the dual station at the very back—we're not exactly star pupils given I've never touched a chef's knife in my entire life.

Of course, this culinary class was my suggestion in the first place, but right now, with everyone else already soaking their ampalaya and me still just about to chop it up, I'm starting to think this whole thing was a bad idea.

'Like a double date?' I stare at my half of the bitter gourd and start scraping off its insides. 'I'd like that. I'll set something up?'

'Sure. Would be nice to get to know your childhood tormentors a little better.'

'Look at you, coming out of your I-have-no-friends-and-prefer-to-be-alone shell.' I lay my ampalaya on the chopping board like I'm paying my respects before it dies. 'Getting over your fear of small talk like a pro.'

'And look at you, making future plans with me.' Luca cocks his head at me, standing beside him. 'Does this mean you're planning on keeping me in your life?'

'Before you go,' I say. 'Don't go jotting things down in your planners just yet.'

'You should definitely get one, Kali. A planner. It'll help you set your life on track.'

'If you're talking about your minimalist, super plain ones, no thanks. Now chop up your ampalaya so I can slack off on mine.'

'Before I go,' he mimics, then proceeds to cut tiny slices of ampalaya on his chopping board.

Luca fills his stainless basin with tap water from the faucet and adds two teaspoons of rock salt to the mix. Then, he whips out his phone from his apron's front pocket and sets the timer. 'Need help with yours?'

'I got this.' I take a deep breath. It's not that I'm afraid of sharp edges or anything—I just feel like I'm clumsy enough to cut myself even if I'm not trying. I slice the ampalaya in slow motion until I get to the very end, my brows knit in pure concentration, extremely aware of Luca staring at me the whole time. Our dual station has two tabletop induction cookers, two sinks, and a working space lined up side by side, and right now, my half of the table is a complete mess.

Luca, on the other hand, has a pristine workspace because he's just too perfect. His diced garlic, ginger, and onions are sitting in their own little bowls to the side with the soy sauce, sesame oil, corn starch, and water already portioned per cup. Meanwhile, all I have is a countertop littered with veggies and bottles of unopened condiments. When I told Luca I wanted to learn how to cook, this wasn't what I had in mind.

'We should've stayed home and watched YouTube instead,' I grumble as soon as I'm done with my ampalaya. 'Remind me again why I'm trying to cook my own food here?'

'Because it'll taste so much better when you've poured your blood, sweat, and tears into it,' Luca chuckles. 'You're just like my mom—always averse to the kitchen.'

'Prepare your marinade with the ribeye sukiyaki on your tray,' the instructor bellows up front. 'You can choose to trim the fat for your ampalaya con carne depending on your preference.'

'So your father's in charge of the food at home?' I try to clear out the chaos on my countertop to no avail. 'That's super cool.'

'He used to be. He'd be wrapped in smoke and oil in the back kitchen while my mother would entertain the guests in the dining area,' Luca smiles at the memory. 'She might not be the one doing the dirty work, but she's got the charm down pat. I think you'd get along well with her.'

'Not one to shy away from the small talk?'

'She thrives when she does it.' Luca rewards me with a sideways smile. 'I'd like for her to meet you sometime.'

We both fall silent after that, knowing full well that's just not going to happen. Luca busies himself with his marinade for a while as his last line hovers over us, and I try not to pull on that dangerous thread.

I clear my throat. 'I guess you're lucky to dodge that bullet with your parents. They sound pretty cool.'

'They are,' he says. 'I'm assuming yours go way back with Uncle Drew too?'

'Pretty much. My mom and Uncle Drew weren't the closest siblings and their mother—I call her Gua-ma—didn't make things any easier for the family dynamics. She always thought Uncle Drew was throwing his life away playing games. It didn't help that he ran away from home when he was my age.'

'That's rough. How did your mom take it?'

'What?'

'Uncle Drew running away,' Luca tilts his head. 'That couldn't have been easy for her, seeing her younger brother leave like that. Could it?'

'I—' I bite my lip. I've been so focused on hating my mother that I never stopped to think how she feels about all this. 'She didn't care, I guess. I mean, she never talked to me about their childhood much.'

'Well . . . siblings can be a tricky thing, too, I suppose.'

'Yeah. Do you have any brothers and sisters?'

'Just me. That's our generation's trend now, I think. I guess having too many kids just isn't practical anymore, but I do wish I had a younger brother I could show the ropes to. Or bully.' Luca rinses his hands after soaking his beef in the marinade. 'You?'

'Same. My parents always wanted a boy, though. Some twisted cultural thing.' I shrug. 'I guess it explains why they've always been disappointed in me.'

Luca tucks my hair behind my ear as I lean over my counter to whip up my marinade. 'Having a boy doesn't automatically mean they've hit the jackpot. Take me, for example—I'm not exactly a golden child.'

'It is what it is.' I start soaking my beef too and shrug. 'Would be nice to have an older sibling, though. Someone my parents can obsess over instead.'

'I guess an older brother would be cool, too. Someone to keep me from making stupid decisions.'

'Like this cooking class?' I rinse my hands and grin at him, but he keeps his intense gaze locked into my eyes.

'Like agreeing to let go of this beautiful girl in front of me when I leave.'

He smiles at me then, but it's tinged with something else, and I have to pretend like his words don't faze me, don't make me feel like dying and breaking down in the middle of a culinary session with random strangers and soggy ampalaya.

'Speaking of bad decisions,' the art of deflection has become second nature to me now, 'what's up with this, then?' I reach out and thumb the stud on Luca's left ear, and he chuckles.

'A silly pact my friends and I made in high school. There were five of us, and we thought we were cool when we were anything but.' Luca rubs his fingers over the earring. 'That was a long time ago, though. We've . . . lost touch since then.'

'Oh.' I tune out the instructor as he starts his next round of instructions up front. 'What happened?'

'Life happened. My father had a stroke, and I started moving forward—I think I moved so fast and so far away that I left them all behind.' Luca shrugs. 'Another bad decision.'

'Luca. You can still reach out to them, you know. It's not too late.'

'Maybe. But all I have is my family now, which is why I'm heading back home,' he says. 'And you, if you want to be a part of it. *Diri ra unta ka, ayaw kawala.*'

Luca whispers the last line in his regional dialect. I don't dare to ask what it means because he looks at me with a sad smile, making everything about this heartbreak I've gotten myself into much, much worse.

'I guess what I'm saying is that this loneliness caused by your family . . . it doesn't have to be yours alone. We can share it, if you want to.'

* * *

'Pass the mangoes please, Kali.'

I take the plastic container with sliced mangoes to my right and hand it over to my mother the next night, and she scoops a few slices onto her plate with a curt 'thank you'. Meals at the Ang household have never been particularly warm, not just in terms of the atmosphere but also in terms of the actual food. My parents have perfected the art of leaving me just the right amount of money to help me get by on my own, and on very, very rare nights when they're both home, it's just packed meals in microwavable containers that have neither the colours nor the life that a proper family meal should.

I guess I don't mind. Uncle Drew was the only one who brought that colour and warmth to this household whenever he came and ate with me to make sure I wasn't alone. Now that he's gone, the whitewashed meals and faded flavours are pretty on-point.

'How's that part-time job of yours?' My father peers above his phone screen, on which he's busy sending emails or whatever it is he does day in and day out. 'They paying you okay?'

I shrug at him from across the dining table. 'It's okay.'

'And college?' My mom pipes in to my left, not a single pleat out of place on her pristine white blouse.

'It's okay too,' I lie.

'Good,' she says then turns back to her mangoes. My father parrots the same word back at me, then promptly goes back to his phone.

Conversations always go like this, and it's not like they honestly care. Asking me how my day went is just a template, a thing to cross off their to-do list so they can get back to more important things.

I finish the rest of my meal without saying anything else, keeping my head down as the quiet tinkling of silverware fills this house of silence. While they both have the liberty of using their devices at the table *for work*, I'm not allowed to do that same, condemning me to this tension-filled fate of rushing through meals just so I can get them over with.

It didn't use to be this bad. My parents run their own electronics business that keeps their hands full, but despite them being away from home most of the time, Uncle Drew's presence somehow felt like the glue that was holding us together. It all came apart the day he died, though, and the void he left in his wake has been growing ever since.

The shrill ring from Mom's phone buzzes the house alive, and I watch as my mother excuses herself to answer the call, no doubt from another one of their business partners or suppliers or clients. I take that as my cue to get up and start clearing the plates, and Dad starts doing the same. There are no clear-cut roles here, not with both of them working full-time. Any one of them washes the dishes, does the laundry, or does all the usual household chores, but while I feel like my folks are pretty progressive when it comes to traditional gender roles, their parenting skills can use a little work.

'Go ahead, Kali.' My father nods at me to give me permission to leave the dishes to him, so I nod and head up to my room. There's nothing left to do down there. I've long ago learned not to linger on the fact that Dad used to say, 'Go ahead, sweetie,' before Uncle Drew's absence twisted everything into our version of an alternative universe.

I guess this is another reason why I just can't see myself cheering for anything anymore. There's no cheer left in me now, and I don't think it will ever return.

That Tiny Sliver of Hope

The miniature bubble tea cup looks foreign and out of place in my hand, the LEGO piece glinting at me like it knows it shouldn't be here. I've never touched LEGO in my life, so I'm not too sure what I'm even doing here, kneeling on the floor of my room with a litter of LEGO bricks around me.

Thankfully, I've got my own expert builder right here, sitting on the floor across from me with his brows creased in total concentration. I found this particular set super cute the day of Luca's LEGO meet-up, and it was sweet of him to buy it for me. He wanted us to build it together, but honestly, he's been laying every single brick without my help this whole time.

'I just don't get it.' I flip through the little manual and frown at the supposedly kid-friendly instructions. 'It all seems like some kind of alien language to me.'

Luca chuckles. 'The box says it's for ages six and above.'

'The box lies.'

'Does it?' He pieces together another chunk of our mobile bubble tea shop. 'It's a good thing your friendly neighbourhood LEGO geek has come to the rescue then, right?'

'My hero,' I lean over to land a quick peck on his cheek. It's a pretty tiny set, and it's got two girls from the LEGO Friends series enjoying their purple-coloured milk tea. As part of Luca's finishing touches, he replaced the two Friends characters with minifigs of a boy and girl in what can pass as barista outfits. They're supposed to be the two of us, sipping our tea and having the time of our lives outside the mobile tea shop.

But not a single vibrant pop of colour from the LEGO set can mask the cloud looming over our heads, the cruel clutches of Time carved onto the four walls of this room and etched right into my heart.

Luca's leaving in two days.

His warmth and scent have latched onto my skin now, but no matter how much I hold onto these fleeting moments and smiling milk tea mascots, I know I'm just trying to scrub myself raw of something that won't go away.

'There you go.' Luca props up his knee and rests his arm on it, admiring his handiwork. 'Set number 41733 done.'

'It's adorable,' I say. 'No thanks to me.'

'Nawww. You did put *one* brick in there.' He grins. 'Every single one counts. One brick at a time.'

'If you say so.' I lean back against him, and I hate that the crook between his legs and his arms seems perfectly carved to fit me. 'What's next?'

'What do you want to do?' His eyes survey my room and land back on mine. 'I do want to point out, for the record, that your bed's right here . . . '

I elbow him in the ribs.

'What?' He laughs, rubbing his chest at the point of impact. 'I'm just saying.'

'I've had enough of a workout today, thanks.' I mock-pout at him, and he coaxes me back into his embrace. Luca's been doing yoga—or trying to—with me in the morning whenever he has the time, and he has a *lot* of time these days. With him no longer scrambling to fit every single book into every hour of his day, Luca's only ever preoccupied with either Tea for Two or me.

That is, until he leaves.

I shake that last thought off my mind. To torture me even further, Luca rests his chin on my right shoulder and starts nibbling on my ear.

I sigh. 'If you don't stop doing that, we might not even make it to the bed.'

'Good.' Luca's low voice rumbles in my ear, and my stomach twists into knots again. I turn and kiss him, tasting every bit of loneliness until we both sigh into each other, helpless and defeated. I gently tug at his lower lip with my teeth before we part, and he sighs again.

'Thank you for forcing your way into my life,' he murmurs.

'Thank you for hiring me,' I giggle. 'Hang on. Did you hire me on the spot because you liked me? That's power-tripping, you know.'

'I hired you because you were passionate and determined. Any side effects of said employment are purely coincidental.' He shrugs. 'Besides, you were coming on to me first. I wouldn't have made a move if you hadn't.'

'*Excuse me?*' I crinkle my nose at him. 'When did I ever come on to you?'

'You asked me to do it with you.' He smirks. 'Yoga.'

I turn red. 'Well, you took me on a campus tour and had ramen with me.'

'I was being nice,' he says. 'You made me sit still for half an hour to drink your tea.'

'*I* was being nice. You looked overworked.'

'Freyja said I was cute.'

'That was on her!' I shove his arm and he chuckles. 'And if you're still dwelling on that then you certainly think highly of yourself.'

'I wasn't trying to be cute. She said that out of pure observation.'

I roll my eyes. 'You took me to a supply run and almost kissed me.'

'I—' A flutter of pink taints Luca's cheeks, and he fires me a lopsided smile. 'You got me there. I didn't mean for that to happen—I didn't mean for *any* of this to happen. I just . . . I couldn't resist you. I'm sorry if I made you feel uncomfortable at any point.'

'You didn't.' I bite my lip. 'To be honest, the first time I saw you, I . . . already thought you were cute.'

'Huh.' Luca tilts his head. 'So you applied for the job thinking you could seduce me? *Now* who's power-tripping?'

'Get out of my room.'

'I'm kidding!' Luca laughs and wraps his arms around me again, pulling me closer. 'I like you, Kali. So damn much. The only reason I didn't try anything was because I never in a million years thought I could ever have a chance with you, so it was the farthest thing on my mind when I hired you. But even if you'd shown the slightest bit of interest, I still would've tried. You're worth the heartbreak.'

'Hmm cheesy, but I'll take it.' I lick my lips and smile. 'Come get your reward, then . . . '

He kisses me again, this time running his hands down my back and tugging my whole body even closer. I shift my position until I'm straddling him, then I push him on his back on the floor and he grunts.

It's a different kind of grunt though, so I pull away.

'Ow ow ow—' Luca winces, reaches behind him to whatever's poking his back, then pulls out the two LEGO Friends figures he had replaced with the minifigs. We stare at each other for a second before we burst out laughing.

'LEGO on the floor is always a poking hazard.' He sits up as soon as I get off him, and we settle in for another embrace.

I nod to our LEGO set. 'Will you be adding this little boba shop to your glorious collection?'

'Of course not. This is *your* set.' He gestures at the two figures chilling on the floor in front of us. 'Besides, that's me and you right there. It'll help you remember me.'

Luca's voice falters just a teeny tiny bit at that last line. I wouldn't have caught it if I hadn't been fixating on it more than I should.

'What about this one?' I pick up the second LEGO set from our mini-haul that day, a mobile coffee cart with a looming coffee cup sign and a charming barista behind the counter.

Luca shakes his head. 'You'll build that one on your own.'

'No way.'

'One brick at a time, Kali. You'll figure it out.'

I sigh. 'Now that you've got more free time, will you finally be able to build all your sets when you get back home?'

'I hope so—at least until I retake the exam,' he shrugs, trying to mask his earlier vulnerability. 'It's not just the time, though. Where am I ever going to find the space to put them all up on display?'

'You've managed okay so far,' I grin. As promised, Luca showed me photos of his LEGO collection back home on his phone—a shelf dedicated to all things brick, with another stash of unbuilt sets in his closet just waiting to be opened. He said he's been trying to cut back on a pretty expensive hobby mainly because there's just no space left. 'Although, given how many unopened boxes you have, I can't imagine how you'll get through them all.'

'Hey, one brick at a time,' he beams down at me. 'It's a bit of a personal motto too. You know, in life.'

'Life lessons from LEGO. Brilliant.' I giggle. 'And your parents don't mind the mess?'

'LEGO isn't a *mess*. LEGO is LEGO.' He tries to act like he's offended but fails. 'And no, they don't. My mom's mostly away in the shop anyway, and Dad's either asleep in his room or tending to his flowers in the backyard. I keep my sets to myself.'

Luca tugs at his earring, and a tiny sliver of discomfort wedges itself between us. 'He needs to take it easy now, my father. Can't risk exhausting him too much again.'

I snake my hand over to Luca's, and he offers me his open palm. 'What are your parents like?'

'Contrary to what others might think, they're pretty cool. People look at me and think I ran away from home to escape some sort of trauma, and in a way, maybe I did. Dad's stroke scarred me pretty badly, and I guess the fear of life stopping just like that propelled me to move and keep moving.' Luca's voice grows softer. 'I guess I was just afraid that if I kept still, time would catch up with me—it would catch up with all of us.'

He looks down. 'It's a good life. The coffee shop is doing okay, Mom and Dad are fine, and as an only child, I never felt like I was in want of anything. I guess I was so focused on looking forward, I never stopped to appreciate what I already have.'

Luca smiles at me then, squeezing my hand. 'Thank god this milk-tea sipping half-hour-sitting whirlwind of a girl slammed her resume on my counter one day and showed me the error of my ways.'

I roll my eyes to stifle the giddiness radiating from my chest. 'Geez. You make me sound like I'm a rom-com manic pixie dream girl come to fix everything wrong about your brooding, colourless life.'

'Of course not.' He sneaks a quick peck on my forehead. 'But I won't say no to the colourless protagonist. Those high-strung career women who always end up finding love in old-school rom-coms after being softened by a live-life-to-the-fullest guy? That's me. I'm the high-strung career woman.'

'Are you kidding me?' I giggle. 'You're telling me I'm Hugh Grant to your Julia Roberts? Mark Ruffalo to your Reese Witherspoon? Ryan Reynolds to your Sandra Bullock?'

Luca shifts away from me and folds his arms across his chest. 'Okay, first of all, what? You blurted out that list of actors from movies of a very, very specific trope insanely fast. Second, aren't those films a little old for you? And third,' his lips curl into a wry smile, 'you forgot Meg Ryan and Hugh Jackman.'

'Uncle Drew likes them, so they're classics to me. We binged a lot of Netflix whenever the folks were away.' I narrow my eyes at him. 'What's *your* excuse?'

Luca answers without missing a beat. 'An ex.'

'Care to elaborate?'

'There's nothing to elaborate. She was a lit major, I wasn't. We met through a common friend and we were okay until we weren't. She just woke up one day and realized she didn't like me as much as she used to anymore, and the weirdest thing was that when she told me, I was okay with it,' he says. 'Sorry it's not as juicy as you were probably hoping.'

'Oh. That common friend who introduced you both totally dropped the ball there.'

'She did. That common friend was Lee.' Luca chuckles at my bewildered expression. 'Yes, Lee's a LEGO goddess, but her matchmaking skills suck.'

'Wow,' I shake my head. 'It all makes sense to me now.'

'Why she's very protective of me? She has to be. She owes me for those two years I wasted on her friend.' Luca shifts and wraps his arms around me again, his voice softening. 'I'm not wasting a single second now, though. I want you to know I'll cherish every moment with you. Before I go.'

And there it is again. Those three words that should've held a promise but hold nothing more than heartbreak now. If I pretend that they don't exist, will they hurt me less?

'We should probably go to work. What time did you say our meeting with the landlord was?'

He smirks. 'Four. And you do know your boss isn't going to mark you down for this, right?'

'I know, *sir.*' I nudge him again, glancing over at my desktop, which I hardly ever turn off. After Frey's live stream and Ryan's academic acrobatics with the principal, my petition now has a solid extra 200 signatures, and I'm feeling pretty confident about presenting all our hard work to the landlord. 'I just . . . miss Uncle Drew today. I wanted to show him the signatures before the meeting.'

'Right. He was a no-show yesterday too, wasn't he?' Luca cocks his head. 'Do you ever wonder where he floats off to when he's not at the shop?'

'I asked and he has no clue, either,' I say. 'It's just . . . I worry he's going to slip away every day.'

'Kali.' Luca fidgets with his earring for a bit. 'Have you ever thought of maybe going about this some other way?'

'What do you mean?'

'You're not gonna like it.'

'I can take it.'

'I just think you've been so focused on keeping him here—maybe you should try thinking about how to make him go away.'

I stare at him for a while. 'You're right.'

His eyes widen. 'I am?'

'Yes. You're right that I don't like what you just said.'

Luca chuckles. 'I have nothing against Uncle Drew, but maybe we should start considering what we can do to help him move on, instead of making him stay.'

'If you're thinking about that "unfinished business" crap, you're wrong, okay?' I grit my teeth. 'He's happy here. He said so himself.'

'I know, but maybe there's something else here. It's just that you're treating him like he'll be there forever and talking to him like you would in a normal, everyday conversation. I'm just saying maybe you should start asking him the important questions and telling him the things you never got to say.'

I don't reply, and Luca immediately senses the shift in the air.

'Okay, I'm sorry I brought it up.' He smiles to put me at ease. 'And about his disappearing acts, I wouldn't worry. He probably has some afterlife stuff to get to as well, you know? But just in case you're ready to help him move on, do it one brick at a time.'

I roll my eyes, and he kisses the top of my head. 'Alright. I'm getting out of these sweats . . .' He gets up off the floor and heads into my bathroom but not before turning back to me by the doorway, ' . . . unless you want to do the undressing for me?'

I chuck the empty LEGO box at him and he ducks into the bathroom, the ghost of his laughter lingering in the room with me. My eyes hover around the two baristas on the floor in front of me, with their plastered-on smiles and their bubble tea in hand, having the time of their lives like Time isn't against them.

I stare at them and they stare right back, judging me with their plastic faces and wondering why I'm letting this good a thing go.

* * *

When the landlord barges into Tea for Two at half past three the next day, the chime over the door suddenly chirps out something that's less cheery than usual. I'm caught halfway between prepping the cash register and wanting to retreat to the back room to fool around with Luca a little bit more, but the presence of a short, middle-aged man in a black sports shirt and white chinos zaps any hormonal urges to oblivion.

I've never seen Mr Valencia save for what Luca's told me about him. But with the sunglasses perched on his head and the way he wears his privilege around him like an overpowering perfume, I immediately pin him as the guy we need to convince to save Tea for Two this afternoon. That, and the fact that he obviously has a key to the shop, seeing as we're still not open and he's half an hour earlier than what we agreed on.

I'm frozen behind the counter when he marches right up to me without a preamble. 'Where's Luca?'

'Mr Valencia!' Luca appears at the doorway to the back room like he's been summoned by an invisible force, and I can tell from the way the initial impish look in his eye was wiped off as soon as he saw the landlord that I wasn't the only one with naughty thoughts just a moment ago. 'You're early, sir.'

'I have another meeting so let's make this quick.'

Time to swoop in. 'I'm Kali, a barista here.' I flash Mr Valencia a smile when he turns his head toward me. 'Would you like to have a seat, sir?'

He sighs. 'Yeah, sure.'

I smile at him again, grab my laptop on the countertop, and lead him to the table right in front of the counter, trying to mask all the nerves firing off in unholy directions inside me. Luca follows suit, and we all pull up chairs across from one another.

'How about a drink, Mr Valencia?' I'm still smiling like it's programmed into my skin. 'Our Assam Milk Tea is—'

'I'm sorry, Kali, but I'm in a bit of a rush.' Mr Valencia lays two smartphones and his car keys on the table. 'Would you both mind telling me what this meeting is about?'

Luca clears his throat. 'I understand, sir, that you're planning on demolishing the establishment by the end of the month?'

'Yes,' Mr Valencia leans back in his chair, 'I have your check, don't I, Luca? I'm not going to start dismantling until your contract's done. You don't have to worry about that.'

'Thank you, sir, but that's not what this meeting is about.' Luca keeps his voice steady, and all of a sudden it's like the Luca I've been hanging out with lately is gone, reverting back to the detached stranger scrutinizing my resume the first day I marched in with full confidence and no skill. 'We were hoping you'd consider saving the building.'

Finally, a crease forms on Mr Valencia's forehead— the first sign of any emotion in his can't-be-bothered face. 'Excuse me?'

'We've been collecting signatures for the past few weeks, sir.' I flip open my laptop and turn it toward him on the table. 'People have been signing this petition to save this space—it's got memories, and no matter how many times the actual store changes, it's still a haunt.' *In more ways than one*, I want to add.

'You made a *petition*?' Mr Valencia narrows his eyes at the screen in front of him. I definitely went all out with this one, probably going overboard beyond just showing him the results of my petition. I laboured over my presentation slides—*slides*, for god's sake—too much last night like I was prepping for a thesis defence, when I haven't even experienced a thesis defence myself.

But I've got my notes memorized and my spiel in place, and I'm not going to let it all go to waste. 'Yes, sir. You see, regular patrons have been coming to this place for decades.' I switch to the next slide to show him a collage of photos of what each establishment here used to be before landing on its current state—Tea for Two. 'And here we have comments that people have left on the petition page, how each and every customer has made memories here, whether that's meeting up with friends after school or studying for a final exam until the wee hours of the night.'

I click to the next slide just as Luca throws me a reassuring smile. 'There's nostalgia in these walls, sir, and a significant number of people agree. If you choose to demolish this place, those evocative feelings will disappear and so will customers' memories with them.'

I click to the next slide with the full results of the online petition. 'I've taken the liberty of sending you these slides via email too, sir, so you can check them at your most convenient time,' I beam at him, but it's at this point that Mr Valencia holds up a hand.

'Kali. I see what you're trying to do here but with this presentation alone,' he shakes his head, 'did you think this was a school project?'

My heart drops. 'No, sir, I—'

'It's a *petition*, Kali. You're hoping to save this building with a petition?' Mr Valencia adjusts the shades on his head. 'Do you even know why I'm tearing this place down?'

Luca tries to do some damage control. 'Mr Valencia—'

The landlord holds his hand up to Luca. 'A potential client wants a long-term lease on the property. Do you both know what the running rates are for real estate these days? It's absurd, but what's even more absurd is having a two-storey structure in a corner lot of a prime location selling snacks or tea or whatever the next tenant decides to do.'

Mr Valencia shakes his head and lets out a small chortle. 'That client wants to maximize the vertical space here and build a five-storey commercial establishment, and that's a lot of money for me. All that's standing in the way is this shop. Their only condition is for me to demolish this thing, which is absolutely what's going to happen.'

A black cloud descends over me. It washes away all the rainbow-coloured hopes and childish whims of random signatures from random people because it's not that simple and this is real life and this is how cruel the actual adult world can be.

My presentation shines with a hopeful glow on my screen, my school logo and slides template plastered on the thing in my desperate attempt to make it seem more official. They glare up at me with all the vibrant colours like they're mocking me. 'You're just a kid,' they seem to say. 'There's nothing you can do to save this place.'

There's nothing I can do to save Uncle Drew.

Upon delivering that harsh dose of reality, Mr Valencia seems to sense how my plastered-on smile has been ripped right off my face. He sighs. 'Look, I understand you might want to keep this because of some high school party or group date your friends might have had here or whatever. In an ideal world, your petition might have worked. But it's not a historical landmark, and business is business. It's all about the bottom line, do you understand? It's just not practical for me to keep the building when it can be so much more. I'm sorry.'

Defeat latches onto my heart and squeezes it. 'No, it's okay, sir. I'm . . . I'm sorry for wasting your time.'

Mr Valencia tilts his head at me for a few more beats—this time, it's the kind of adult head tilt that doesn't sympathize about death but about the cluelessness of youth. Then, he shakes his head again and pushes back his chair. 'Well, if there's nothing else—'

'Actually, Mr Valencia, there is.'

Luca's firm tone makes both Mr Valencia and I turn toward him. I blink away the veil of disappointment in my eyes, looking at Luca like I just remembered he was there.

'If you're talking about the bottom line, this space has a lot of untapped potential,' Luca goes on even as Mr Valencia looks like he's tolerated our nonsense enough. 'I've checked, sir. These walls are in fantastic condition, and the structural integrity of the building is intact. Even if you strip it down to its parts, you can still salvage a great deal of materials here, but why sell for scrap when you can just renovate and revive the place?'

Mr Valencia folds his arms across his chest but doesn't say anything.

'The foundation is solid, sir. You won't have to spend too much beyond a minor facelift. If you're leasing this out as a commercial building, imagine how much more you can make with something that's your own.' Luca is on a roll. 'And I'm not asking you to turn down that client—that would be stupid. All I ask is that you at least postpone your decision and think about it.'

Luca's done. The silence in the shop imposes upon all of us, and the worst part of it all is that even though he's out of sight all the way over in his corner booth, I know that Uncle Drew has heard the entire thing.

But despite my frazzled nerves and the heat threatening to burst from my eyes, Mr Valencia sighs for the nth time. Then, he nods at Luca. 'As much as I hate to admit it, you have a point.' Mr Valencia grabs his phones and keys on the table and makes a move to stand up. 'I'll have my guy inspect the place and look into what you're saying. I guess it can't hurt to delay the demolition for another week.'

'Thank you, sir.' Luca stands with Mr Valencia and so do I, still in a daze and still with no idea about what just happened. He gives Mr Valencia a firm handshake. 'We appreciate it.'

'Thank you for your time, Mr Valencia.' I offer him a handshake as well, and he takes it.

He doesn't say anything else as he leaves the shop and drags all the discomfort along with him. As soon as he's out of sight, Luca turns to me.

'Kali, I'm so sorry. It's the best I could—'

'Thank you.' I smile up at my civil engineer-in-the-making, and the moment his eyes soften at me, all the disappointment somehow starts to melt away. 'I should've known the petition wouldn't work. But what you did at least gave us a fighting chance, and that tiny sliver of hope matters more than you know.'

Luca's silence makes me realize that what I just said doesn't just apply to Tea for Two. The pulse of hurt that sails across his features clutches at my heart again, snuffing out any fleeting remnants of happiness.

Luca's leaving tomorrow—it will be his last day with me.

Despite everything that just happened or didn't happen between us, I've somehow managed to snatch away that sliver of hope for him, declaring with a cruel finality that he's not even worth that fighting chance.

But if it hurts him as much as it hurts me, he doesn't say anything. All he does is take my hand and give me a smile laced with pain.

He kisses the top of my hand. 'I'll hold on to that tiny sliver of hope then,' he says, 'for as long as I can.'

All Kinds of Misery

Luca's last day is coloured a perpetual shade of orange, with hints of purple and blue seeping in like we're frozen in time. Even though the sun is scorching hot and high up in the sky, it almost feels like twilight has already woven its magic over the world. There's an unsettling of sorts, a humming inside my body that just can't help itself, a telltale sign that deep down, my body is prepping for the kind of heartbreak I might not recover from.

Every move Luca makes is tinted with sadness, every word another chip that eats away at my heart. I hate that this blanket of loneliness is ruining what's supposed to be our last day together, but who am I kidding?

I made this decision. I have no one to blame but myself.

'Everything should be in here.' Luca stuffs the photocopies of Tea for Two's documents inside a folder as soon as the attendant hands us our papers. The final stop of our so-called magical last day isn't even made for us— it's a trip to the copy place here at the local mall, Luca's last-minute attempts to give me everything I need for that one-week extension I have after he's gone.

'You don't have to keep the place running, you know.' Luca licks his lips as I take the folder from him inside the copy place. 'You can just spend the whole week with your uncle and keep Tea for Two closed. The rent's paid up anyway.'

'Thanks. I'll think about it.' We both shuffle out of the shop and start trekking down the bridgeway to the station. It's the same place I always go to, but when we pass by all the stores Uncle Drew and I used to haunt, somehow, his absence doesn't seem so big. Luca leaving is contributing to most of the weight in my chest now, and it's getting worse as we get closer to the end.

'Are you hungry?' he asks as soon as we're along the strip of food kiosks lining the hall to the ticket barriers. 'We can grab a bite first if you like.'

I scan the mishmash of colours and smells and sights and sounds at the station, the passengers in a rush and the students playing hooky and the frenzy of the hungry crowd. Everything from the finger-staining, cheese-flavoured French fries to the greasy fish balls dipped in unholy concoctions should cause sensory overload, but all my mind can focus on is the muted white noise inside my chest, that tiny frequency tuned to Luca and Luca alone, and the looming anxiety of him leaving. Grabbing a bite to eat almost feels like we're stalling, delaying the inevitable with a sinful bite and an unsatisfied appetite.

I swallow the lump in my throat. 'A cup of coffee would be nice.'

The sideways smile. 'You do know that we work in a cafe, right?'

'I know,' I say. 'I just . . . I just want to hang out for a while.'

'I know,' Luca runs a hand through his hair. 'I do too.'

Two steaming cappuccinos later, we're leaning on the railings at one corner of the station, looking out over the chaos of the city with our cardboard coffee cups in hand. The din of the crowd feels less intrusive here, like we've just hopped off the current in a plea to make Time stop in this little pocket of us.

Luca's eyes twinkle as cars and buildings across the city come alive beneath us. There's a wayward strand of hair casually grazing his left cheek, and I fight the urge to brush it away.

'What do you plan to do when the week's over?' He takes a sip from his coffee without looking at me.

'I'm not sure,' I sigh. 'I haven't thought it through. I guess I'll just try and spend as much time as I can with Uncle Drew with what little I have.'

'Mr Valencia might still change his mind, you know,' Luca says. 'It's a long shot, but he just might.'

'Maybe, maybe not. But I don't want that kind of anxiety to ruin the time I have left.'

At this, Luca turns to me and the desperation in his eyes mars me. 'It doesn't have to be that way.'

I blink at him. 'What?'

'The helplessness. The waiting around until someone leaves. Before *I* leave.' He rests his coffee on the ledge of the railing and takes my hand in his. 'Kali. I know I said I didn't want to ask you to stay with me despite the distance, but I . . . I think we can. I think we should.'

Luca's voice softens to almost a whisper, but even in the thunderstorm of the station, his voice is all I can hear. 'I want to be with you, Kali. This . . . what we have . . . it doesn't have to end. All I ask is that you please think this through.'

The white noise in my chest hums louder now, bigger and wilder and frantic and scared, until the drumming starts to hurt. It's the smell of freshly brewed tea and scattered engineering books and aprons in the back and sitting still for thirty minutes and chicken tinola and the Batman sticker on the laptop, all crushed and packed and rolled into this cold, metal ball, mercilessly weighing down my chest.

Something hot and painful scrambles its way out of my throat and scalds the back of my eyelids at the same time, and it's my reply, my two words, my way of scarring Luca with as much cruelty as I'm scarring myself.

'I can't.'

The two words that tumble out of my mouth wound Luca so much that he actually flinches, and I can almost hear the gasp of pain he's desperately trying to hold back, like my words had the physical impact of knocking the air right out of him. Instead, he tries to force a smile to reassure us both.

'Right. You're all about the here and now, and I'm neither going to be here nor now, so.'

My voice breaks. 'Luca . . . '

He shakes his head, and the hurt on his face is gone. 'It's okay, Kali. I knew this about you from the start, and only an idiot thinks they can change someone in a relationship from being who they really are.' He smiles at me again. 'I'm sorry I brought it up.'

I struggle to find anything else to say to him but come up with nothing. We both finish our coffee in silence.

After a few more minutes in our pocket of universe outside of time, Luca chucks our empty coffee cups into a nearby bin and smiles. 'Ready to go?'

I nod. He takes my hand and we merge right back into the current, because life isn't all sunshine and rainbows and milk tea and LEGO sets. It's fleeting moments of elusive happiness, sudden deaths in the corner of a coffee shop and parents who don't care and friends going to separate colleges and failed boards exams and empty coffee cups in trash bins and plastic Cheetos pendants that are a poor excuse of the real thing.

As the doors of the train close behind us, Luca wraps an arm around me and coaxes me into his body to shield me from the tightening crowd. There are no other stops in Time's own express train now, so I lay my head against Luca's chest and close my eyes, preserving this fragile moment before that train takes him away and leaves me behind.

* * *

Luca hands me a tiny envelope with no label on it as soon as I get off at my stop, telling me not to open it until his train is out of sight. We could've lingered longer at the station, but he needed to get home and return his car—or Lee's car, apparently—that he borrowed for his brief stint here in Manila before his flight back to Cebu. Plus, we both decided it was best if we didn't text or call before he left.

'Before I go,' he whispered and gave me one final kiss before it all ended. It was all I could do not to burst into tears right then, so when we parted, all I did was smile at him before I got off my stop. Any longer and I would've broken down and begged him to stay with me, which isn't going to do either of us any good.

The rest of the way home is a blur. I take a deep breath to steel myself outside my door, then step inside our house for another round of oppressive silence.

But as soon as I close the door behind me, I can already tell that something's very, very wrong.

When Uncle Drew was alive, we were the only ones who ever used the living room. We'd lie on the two single-seater sofas that we'd nudge together to form one big one, and I'd mess around with the backs of the sofas for a bit until I found the right angle. It was one of those manual reclining things that are cheaper versions of the automatic ones, and Uncle Drew had long ago removed the armrests so that the two sofas would merge into one.

We'd scatter our stuff around the small table and I'd prep my laptop for a Netflix rom-com marathon after school, whether it's enemies to lovers or friends to lovers or childhood friends-turned-something else. Whenever Uncle Drew left, he'd take all the life and the mess with him, and the living room would once again be what it's always been—a pristine display set no one ever touched, not a single reclining back out of place, not a pillow in disarray.

Now, though, now it's different. There are some personal effects scattered on the table, notes, keys, some hand sanitizer, and, most importantly, Mom's phone.

She's home.

And she's in my room.

I dash up the stairs and find her right where I don't want her to be, standing in front of my computer with my monitor wide open and the petition on full display for all the world to see. She's staring down at my screen with a look of horror in her eyes, and for a second, I almost recognize the passionate spark her brother always had in his.

But my Mom's gaze has nothing enchanted about it, no hopes of Netflix rom-coms or XL Cheetos bags, of guild battles on my phone or unlimited cabbage salads at the mall.

All that's there is disappointment in her eyes, reminding me precisely why we've never been as close as we should be.

'Mom, I—'

'Kali.' She fixes her soulless gaze at me, and her perfectly pleated pantsuit actually has a wrinkle on it. 'What is this *garbage*?'

I grit my teeth to stifle my indignation. Her poor choice of words, as always, ruins a conversation before it can even start. 'It's not *garbage*, Mom. It's a petition I made to save a local tea shop.'

'I know what it is. I've read the petition you've apparently been working so hard on.' Mom's glare doesn't let up. 'What I mean is why you're wasting your time saving a building from demolition when all you should be thinking about is college.'

'I'm not wasting my time. This is important to me, which is something you've never understood.'

'Excuse me?'

'This is important to me,' I repeat more slowly this time, trying my hardest not to let my anger get the best of me. 'I *need* to save this building.'

'No, you don't. What you *need* is to get into a good college. Shut this down. Now.'

'No.'

'No?'

'No!' I clench my fist. 'Why are you even in my room in the first place? Shouldn't you be off not caring about me?'

My mother raises her chin in a way that tells me she's had enough. Looking at the way her nostrils are flaring, I know there's a pent-up tirade she wants to unleash on me right now.

'I'm here because Principal Siy called.'

What.

'She gave my contact number to a certain Mr Valencia, who saw your school template on your nonsensical *slides* and wasn't sure how to deal with this like a proper adult should. I'm here because you're a *teenager* and he was looking for the right *adult* to discuss this with, because you have *no business* meddling in other people's affairs just because you want to keep a worthless tea shop from closing.'

And there it is. Today is just *not* a good day, and I can't deal with this shit.

'I'm here because I don't care if you and your friends can't let go of a silly hangout. What I do care about is your university and you leaving all of these meaningless, childish things behind.'

And maybe it's the fact that Luca just left and the petition failed and my two best friends can't go to college together and Uncle Drew is slipping away and my mother has picked this exact moment to pretend she cares, the feigned strength I've been trying to display unravels.

'I can't.'

'Kali Stephanie Ang. You drop all this nonsense this instant and—'

'It's Uncle Drew.'

'What?'

'Uncle Drew.' I whisper to keep the trembling from getting worse. 'I . . . I can see him.'

My mother's eyes widen, and for the first time, she's caught off-guard.

'He's in the shop, Mom. I see him every day, and he can see me, and I can talk to him . . . ' The heat from the back of my eyes has been lingering around since the train station, and a single tear finally breaks through. 'I miss him, Mom, but he's right there, and if I save the shop, I won't have to lose him again.'

The moment of silence that passes between us grows thick with all kinds of misery, and I watch through the haze in my eyes as my mother's face goes through shock and sadness and fear and even more shock in an instant. For a second, I actually think she might come over and hug me in a random bout of insanity. But then she finally decides on anger, and what she says cements the insurmountable distance between us.

'How dare you,' she whispers. 'How dare you use your uncle's death like this.'

'Mom, I swear I—'

'You're going to college. I'm calling your Aunt Iris right now.' She marches past me and her tone drips with tethered fury, so much so that I can feel the rage emanating from her as she brushes past.

'In *Texas*?' I clench my fist. 'Mom! I can't just—'

'You're going to college, and I'm shipping you out of here and this godforsaken tea shop and this godforsaken city. If you have time enough to make up this *trash* about your uncle then you have time enough to pack.' She whips around at me one last time.

'You leave within the week.'

When Will This All Go Away?

Tea for Two looks different to me now. The warmth that cosied up the walls is gone, leaving them cold and dull. The smell of fresh tea leaves isn't as strong as it used to be and even the sounds of the brew whirring away in the background don't sound as alive—not when there's no longer a brooding barista working hard with his books in the back room.

It's been cleared out. The books that were scattered all over the back room are now nowhere to be found, everything as pristine and in place as it should be, no laptop propped up on the table or a lopsided smile or the glinting of a stud earring. There's only the supplies now, tea for a tea shop, and aprons neatly folded in perfect squares like only Luca could do. I don't even dare to head up the stairs—I don't think my heart can take it.

I grab the door frame leading to the back room to steady myself, taking a deep breath. I'm still here. The shop is still here. And I can't let this debilitating loneliness distract me from what I'm here for. The reason why I let Luca go in the first place.

Uncle Drew.

Uncle Drew is still here.

I keep the sign on the shop as 'CLOSED' then stagger to the corner booth, half expecting to not see him, as was the trend of late, and not knowing what I would do if I didn't. But Uncle Drew is sitting right there, the newsboy cap and the unchanging face and the same outfit—the only outfit he'll ever wear.

I miss him so damn much.

'Hey kiddo,' he greets me as soon as I slip into the seat across from him. 'Sorry it didn't go well with the meeting.'

Right, the meeting. Uncle Drew still thinks the meeting with Mr Valencia was the most eventful thing that happened since we last spoke—he has no clue what happens each time he doesn't appear. He only thinks he's moving from one day to the next, and I can't imagine how lonely this kind of existence must be, shuffling from one day to another, all of them the same, all of them in one place.

'Yeah, I should've known the petition wouldn't work.' A clamp latched around my heart when Luca left, and it hasn't really gone away since. 'I honestly don't know what I was thinking.'

'You worked very, very hard, kiddo. You did what you could,' he says. 'It wasn't all for nothing, though. You were so into it. It was nice seeing you be so passionate about something again.'

'That's not the point, Uncle Drew. I want to save you. I want you to stay with me.' I look up at his face just as fear and worry mushroom all over it, and I realize that it's me. I'm crying, somehow and all at once, and I don't even remember when it started. 'And I tried, Uncle Drew. I really tried . . . but now all I have is barely a week left with you, and I can't even see it through.'

Uncle Drew reaches over to hold his hand over mine again, and it just goes right through. I don't even feel a thing, not a tingling sensation, not a cold draft, nothing remotely close to what those ghost stories always show in the movies. There's just his hand passing through mine like a badly Photoshopped photo, and the yearning to feel his hand burns inside my chest.

'Kali,' his voice softens, 'what do you mean? What happened?'

'Mom happened.' I swipe at my eyes with the back of my hand, angry at the memory and angrier that I'm crying about it. 'She found out about this whole thing and decided to ruin my life even more by shipping me off to Texas.'

'To Iris?' Uncle Drew blinks in confusion. 'Didn't she always plan on you studying there?'

'She wanted me to, but I never thought she'd act on it. I don't even know how she's going to manage admissions with whatever clout she has, but she just wants me out of here as soon as possible because I'm apparently wasting my life.' I grit my teeth as my voice breaks. 'I'm . . . I'm leaving soon, Uncle Drew. I'm not going to be able to see you anymore.'

Uncle Drew offers me his silence for a while, but then he sighs.

'Maybe that's okay.'

'What?'

'You leaving. Not being able to see each other. Maybe that's okay.' Uncle Drew offers me a smile, but I pull my hand away from the table like he can actually feel it. 'Kali. Maybe that's how things are supposed to be, you know? Maybe . . . maybe I'm not supposed to be with you forever.'

'Don't. Don't say that.'

'Kali, please.' He shakes his head again. 'I don't know what I'm doing here, and if Hollywood is the least bit accurate, I should have some sort of unfinished business to get to before I can move on, right? But I'm still here, and I can't go anywhere else, and you're all I have, Kali. Maybe I'm supposed to stay with you and make sure you're okay and watch over you as long as I can. But now that you're leaving, maybe . . . maybe this is it. Maybe this is as much as I can do for you. Maybe it's as far as I can go.'

He takes a deep breath. 'Maybe it's time to say goodbye.'

'No.'

'Kali—'

'No, Uncle Drew. I'm not saying goodbye when I just got you back in my life. I never got to say goodbye that day and I don't ever want to,' I fight to keep my voice steady, but the fury inside me claws at my chest and begs for release. 'I'm fighting so damn hard to keep you here, and now you're asking me to just *leave*? How can you even say that? How can you be okay with this? How can you give up that easily?'

'I'm not giving up on you, Kali. I would never do that.' He rubs a hand against his forehead and sighs. 'I love you and I want to spend every single hour I have with you, Kali—believe me, I really, really do. But this isn't healthy for you, and I can't let you waste your life here with me.'

'You sound just like your sister.'

'And maybe this time, she's right.' Uncle Drew clenches his jaw. 'Didn't you tell me that Freyja wants to be with Ryan so badly she's giving up her own dream? You're doing the same thing here, Kali. You're holding on to us so badly, you're giving up your own dreams, and I . . . I just think that you should be out there living your life instead of tethering yourself to mine when I'm clearly no longer alive.'

He sighs. 'I'm dead, Kali. There's nothing more you can do for me.'

'Don't you think I know that?' I bite my lip to muzzle the trembling, but the tears fall anyway. 'I *know* you're dead, okay? I know it so damn much that every single thing in my stupid house and my stupid life reminds me of you, and everywhere I go it's always you and your face and your memories with me, and it's not fair that they're the last ones I'll ever have with you, so if I could even have the slightest chance to make more, I would gladly put my life on hold.'

I clench my fist and stand, every single bone in me shaking with rage and frustration and so much sadness.

'I *know* you're dead, Uncle Drew, but what I don't know is *why*, because none of this is fair, and it's not fair that I get to see you now and talk to you when no one else can, and it's not fair that they're taking this place down and I don't know what's going to happen to you because I won't even be here when they do. And the worst part of it all is that, despite all the pain and loneliness and the injustice of it all, *you actually agree with this*, and that breaks my heart most of all.'

The tears come freely now, and I don't even try to mask the pain. Uncle Drew shoots up and makes a move to wrap his arms around me, but I know he can't—he can't leave his booth, and he's stuck here and I'm stuck elsewhere and everything sucks, death sucks, life sucks.

'Kali, I'm so sorry. I'm—'

I don't let him finish. I stomp away from the booth with my stupid tears and my stupid shaking fists and this stupid clamp in my chest. When will this all go away?

That same veil of sadness envelops me in its cold embrace now, more than my Uncle Drew ever could.

Cheetos Are Mankind's Greatest Invention

One Brick at a Time

Twilight finds its way to me again at the circle, on the very same bench and at the very same spot where Luca and I cemented our not-a-relationship that day. I don't know what it is about this particular moment in time, this part of the day where there's either the hope of something new or the loss of what once was.

Given what I've just been through, I'm pretty sure which of the two this time of day means for me.

The Luca-shaped absence beside me gnaws at my edges more violently today, and I don't even know why. This was exactly what I wanted, wasn't it? To live in the here and now, to appreciate the present, to sip the milk tea and not give a damn about the future.

Luca's gone now, and the proverbial milk tea is still here, dull and tasteless.

He did what I wanted. He left and did what I wanted, and I haven't heard a single thing from him since, not a message at the airport or a photo from home or any proof of life I could cling to. It wasn't meant to last forever, nothing is, and now even Uncle Drew will soon fade away. Then Death will welcome me like an old friend, because it knows I have nothing left but this grief in my heart.

When Luca's car pulls into the parking lot across from me, my heart perks up because he's here, he's back, and we can just forget about this whole stupid thing about living in the moment and promises I can't keep. But then Lee emerges from the driver's seat and I'm reminded that it's not actually Luca's car—he's islands away from me now, back with his family and doing something good with his life, away from the mess that is me.

'Hey you.' Lee marches up to me on the bench with that same monotonous drawl befitting Vengeance Incarnate.

'Hey.' I scoot over on the bench to make room for her. 'Sorry for the random message.'

She sits down and shakes her head. 'I'm glad you reached out. Everything okay?'

'Yeah. I just wanted to give you these.' I hand her a small paper bag. 'Just some stuff Luca left at Tea for Two. A planner and a couple of pens.'

'Right.' Lee takes the bag from me and peers into it. 'And you're giving me this, because . . .?'

'Sorry. I don't know any of Luca's other friends. This stuff could be important.'

'This planner is blank.'

'Well—you never know. He has identical ones. Please tell him not to worry.'

'Tell him yourself.'

'I can't.' I turn away to hide the heat burning up my face. 'I . . . sort of promised I wouldn't contact him.'

'Oh my god.' Lee drawls. 'You're both idiots. No offence.'

I turn back at her face then, and somehow, with her super serious expression and her super serious tone, Lee gets through to me. The corners of my lips tug upwards in a small smile. 'None taken. My best friend said the exact same thing.'

'Your best friend is a genius.' Lee sighs. 'Let me tell you this. When he returned my car, I told Luca not to go along with your stupid no-contact rule. He refused—he said you made it clear where you both stood, and that a no means no. He said that gone are the days when persistence from a guy could be seen as romantic. I believe his exact words were, "This isn't a rom-com."'

She shakes her head. 'I know well enough not to meddle in his relationship—I haven't had the best track record of helping him in that area. And I won't pretend I know you well enough to give you any advice. But as I've said before, I'm very protective of my LEGO children, and I want Luca to be happy. So I *will* say this.' She gestures at the paper bag on her lap. 'Whatever it is you're trying to do here, I hope you can at least look at things from the other party's perspective and not just yours. That's all I ask.'

Lee rises and holds the paper bag up. 'I'll keep this with me for the time being to respect your wishes, but I hope you'll give it to Luca yourself someday. After all, a blank planner and a random pen could be important.'

She says the last line with a teeny tiny smirk on her face, and I find myself smiling too.

'Thanks, Lee.' I get up and give her a hug, and she squeezes me back despite the colourless look on her face. Then, with a small wave, Vengeance Incarnate marches back to her car and drives away, leaving me a messier chaos than I was before she arrived.

Looking at things from another person's perspective . . .
not thinking of everything from my own point of view for
once . . . is it possible I should do the same for Uncle Drew?

Was Luca right, then, all this time?

Uncle Drew told me he was happy here, and that he
wanted to spend every moment he had with me. But when
they tear the place down and there's nothing left, the last
memory he'll have is me gone, and he'll think that he never
even made a difference. He'll wonder what the point of him
sticking around was when there was nothing else to do and
nothing else to change. And just like my guilt, thinking it was
my fault he was on the kerb that fateful day, he'll forever be
haunted by the guilt that he had a second chance and never
made anything out of it. All he did was hang out with me
day in and day out, forever living in the moment, forever
unchanging, forever meaningless.

Being in the present is all well and good, but it's the future
to look forward to—that tiny sliver of hope—that gives it
all meaning.

I've been desperately holding on to Uncle Drew from the
very beginning, but it's gotten me nowhere—just a closing
tea shop and a broken heart. Maybe it's not about keeping
Uncle Drew here. Maybe it's more about finding a way to let
him go, no matter how overwhelming it feels. Maybe there's
more than one way to save my uncle.

Maybe it's not all about me.

I take a deep breath then, thumbing the single two-by-
four LEGO brick in my pocket. On Luca's last day, that little
envelope he had for me turned out to be a piece of red brick

and a note that said, 'One brick at a time.' Even when he's not here, he's still trying to help me move on.

A different kind of determination zaps through me now, and maybe it's that same kind of passion and fire Luca said he saw in me when I first marched into the shop.

Don't worry, Uncle Drew, I repeat my mantra to myself. *I'm going to save you if it's the last thing I do.*

Just Like That

'You're back.' Uncle Drew fidgets with his newsboy cap as I slide into the booth the next day. It takes a second for me to get used to his less-than-cheery look. 'I wasn't sure I'd see you again after what I said. I'm so sorry, Kali.'

'No—*I'm* sorry.' I settle into my seat across from him. 'I've been going about this whole thing the wrong way, and it had to take Luca leaving to knock some sense into me.'

'Wait—Luca left?' Uncle Drew frowns. 'What happened?'

I shake my head. 'It's not important. What's important is what he said before he left, and that was to make sure I'm doing everything I can to help you move on. I told you I'd save you, Uncle Drew, and maybe it's not about keeping the building intact. Maybe it's something else.'

'What do you mean?' Uncle Drew bores his gaze into my eyes. 'Kali. What did you do?'

'Kali?'

The voice that wanders in with the door chime pokes at my heart with a different kind of sensation, tickling and tingling and evoking old memories of hot rice porridge on sick days and unlimited candy during fridge raids. I turn around and my grandmother lingers there by the doorway, her short curly hair dyed the wrong shade of brown and her glasses sitting perilously on her nose with a beaded string around her neck holding them in place. She looks shorter than I remember, but no amount of wrinkles on her face can dull the shine her smile radiates when she lands her crinkled eyes on mine.

I stand up. 'Hi, Gua-ma.'

She smiles at the greeting—the Hokkien term for maternal grandmother—and I know she's just glad I haven't foregone that part of my culture just yet. She shuffles over to me and I give her a big hug, bigger than I'd ever done before, if only because I haven't been in touch since Uncle Drew died.

'I came as soon as I got your message.' Gua-ma shakes her head at me, and I gesture for her to take a seat across mine. 'You never text me anymore.'

'I know—I'm sorry.' We both take our seats, and as my Gua-ma settles into hers, I catch Uncle Drew's bewildered face gaping at her beside him. 'I've been doing a lot of stupid things lately . . . but this is important.'

Gua-ma flashes me a gentle smile. 'You do know that I'm supposed to meet your mother today, right?'

'I know. That's why I called you.'

'Ever the troublemaker.' She snickers, and that tiny moment instantly makes me regret not texting her for the longest time. 'So, Kali, what can I do for you?'

'I just want to talk,' I say, 'about Uncle Drew.'

'Kali.' Uncle Drew's tone grows dark. 'What the hell are you doing?'

'Oh.' Gua-ma's smile falters. 'Sure, honey. What about him?'

'All my life, all I've ever heard from Uncle Drew was how at odds you both were, how you never understood him until he ran away.' I keep my fist clenched under the table. 'I want to know your side of the story, Gua-ma.'

Uncle Drew flinches. 'Kali, don't.'

But I power through. 'I want to know what happened.'

At this, my grandmother sighs, making her small frame look even smaller. 'I'm not sure why you want to know *now* after all this time, but . . . ' She folds her hands on the table in front of her. 'He was right.'

She looks down at her hands. 'We were always at odds. He was always slacking off, in school and at work. Always with the wrong kind of crowd, always up to no good.'

Uncle Drew grits his teeth. 'Kali, this is pointless.'

'Your mother tried her best to keep him honest, but all he ever did was go from school to school and girl to girl and job to job without any direction in life. Little Iris did her best not to be like him. And your *Gua-kong*—bless his soul—said it was some sort of middle-child syndrome. He gave up on Andrew before he even ran away.'

Uncle Drew clenches his jaw. This must be torture for him—hearing every bad thing he's ever thought about himself straight from his own mother's mouth. The worst part of it all is that he can't leave—there's nowhere else to go, nothing else to do but sit there and relive his failures and disappointments like they're being read off a checklist.

'So yes, Kali, we never understood him,' Gua-ma goes on, 'but that's not on him.'

Uncle Drew turns to look at his mother.

'We should've fought harder for him, Kali. Should've fought to understand where he was coming from, what he was going through. Should've made an effort to understand that video game job of his that you both loved and bonded over so much . . . ' Gua-ma's lip trembles. 'He did what he could to live his best life, but your Gua-kong and I were too fixated on what was right, what was *proper*, what society would think of a deadbeat son who had no business sense. We were too focused on what other people would think that we didn't even stop to see what our own son would think.'

Her hands start to tremble too, and I reach out to hold my hand over hers. 'The worst part is that I tried so hard to reach out to him after your Gua-kong died, but life always got in the way, until it no longer did.'

'Gua-ma . . . '

'We were wrong, Kali. *I* was wrong. It was all our fault.' She looks up at me. 'I wish I could tell him that, but it's too late now. Too late for any of this . . . '

I stare into her eyes then, just as her tears start to fall, and there, in the middle of my grandmother's soft sobs and the pained look on Uncle Drew's face, I make a decision.

'It's not.'

'I'm sorry?'

'It's not too late, Gua-ma.' I squeeze her hand then turn my gaze to my uncle. 'Uncle Drew is right here beside you.'

'What . . . what are you saying?'

'He's here, Gua-ma. He's always been here. I don't know why, but he's here in this coffee shop every day. I can see him, Gua-ma. He talks to me. And everything you said just now . . . he heard the entire thing.'

In maddening slow-motion, I watch as my grandmother turns her trembling, tear-stricken face slightly to her side, but then the door to Tea for Two slams open and reveals my enraged mother at the doorway, gaping at me.

'Kali!' She stomps over to the booth, her horrified look going from me to her mother and back to me. 'I tell you to drop this stupidity and you bring your own *grandmother* into your *nonsense?*'

I grit my teeth and glare right back up at her. 'This isn't *nonsense*—Uncle Drew is right here—'

My mother grabs my wrist. 'We're leaving. *Now.*'

I wrench myself free of her grip. 'We're *not* leaving! If you could just open your tiny mind just this once, you'd—'

'Enough!' Her gaze flares up at me now, and for once, my mother's properly manicured pose frays around the edges. 'Your uncle is *dead*, do you understand me? He's *dead*, and he's not coming back, and that's so damn irresponsible of him, to up and leave all the broken fragments of his life behind without even bothering to wonder who will pick up the pieces when it all goes to hell. I'll never see him again, not even to scream at him or tell him I'm sorry for being a crap sister, for leaving him my only daughter to build an actual relationship with because I'm too weak to build one myself.'

My mother trembles. 'So don't tell me you can *see* him because he's *gone*, he's gone and he never even said goodbye and . . . and . . .'

My grandmother chooses this exact second to turn to her side again and whisper, silent and loud all at once. 'Andrew.'

Uncle Drew breaks at the sight of his mother looking straight at him even though she can't see him. This time, it's my turn to freeze in place, because right there, in the middle of Tea for Two with her perfect hair and perfect pantsuit and perfect face, my mother unravels.

And she cries.

She cries and as the tears that I'd never seen before stream down her face, I realize that Death is a black hole, a cruel void of emptiness that sucks everything and everyone around it into nothingness for as long as the space where the dead used to be remains. It ruins everything it touches, changes it and twists it into a duller, less full version of itself. It strips all kinds of colours away, and this veil of grief, this thing I've been carrying around with me since that fateful day outside the shop, it's shared, it's expandable, it doesn't have to be mine alone.

My mother buries her face in her hands now, and I can feel her rage clawing out in desperation. I know because that's exactly how I feel.

So, I get up and wrap my mother in a hug, and she sobs even harder.

'He was my brother, and now he's gone,' she whispers in between breaths, and I realize that I'm crying too. 'I miss him so damn much.'

'I know, Mom,' I squeeze her tighter—I never noticed how thin my mother has become. 'I know.'

At this, Uncle Drew's voice breathes through the cafe.

'I forgive them,' he says, 'and I'm sorry too.'

His death maimed us all, and he's the only one who can patch us back together.

I break free from my mother's embrace for a second, happy tears pushing the ugly ones out from my own eyes. 'He says he forgives you, Ma.' I turn to Gua-ma. 'He forgives you both.'

My mother cries even more, and a few more seconds later, Gua-ma rises from her seat and joins the hug fest too, and the three of us stay huddled that way, crying yet giggling because we look too silly but are just too tired to care.

When I lift my head from my mother's shoulder, I look over at Uncle Drew in his seat, tears trickling down his cheeks in silence. His grief is just as palpable, like he's straining in desperation just to reach his family in a moment as vulnerable as this.

But he can't.

* * *

The rest of the day waves an air of relief over the tea shop, like it's finally able to breathe after suffocating for so long in the dark. I spend the afternoon making tea for my mom and my grandmother, reminiscing about the good times and the bad times and everything Uncle Drew ever did to make an irreplaceable dent in our lives. Conversations and laughter flow through every woman in the cafe that day, the CLOSED sign outside Tea for Two a testament to the uninterrupted well of memories being made within.

By the time my mother leads Gua-ma to the door, the sun has already started retiring over the horizon, signalling a temporary end to what I hope will be a new beginning.

Gua-ma cups my cheek and offers me a different kind of head tilt, one that tells me I can spring as far away from her as possible but she'll still always welcome me back and show up at a random tea shop for me with a single text message. Even Mom pauses by the doorway on her way out, hesitates, then asks, 'See you at dinner?'

I smile. 'Sure, Mom.'

'Good.' She smiles back, still pained and manicured, but with a little bit more warmth now. Then, she and Gua-ma take one final look over at the corner booth, and they leave before another bout of sobbing begins.

The air inside the shop weighs itself down with something more familiar now, and I realize that it's Death, and that maybe it hasn't left my side all this while. Tea for Two welcomes back the silence, and now it's Uncle Drew and me, just the two of us.

I slide into the corner booth across from my uncle, and it's all I can do not to reach out across the table, wishing to be in his physical presence one final time. He gazes at me with that impish look on his face, and all of a sudden there's something else there, something finite, something that I know will break my heart.

'Thank you,' he says.

'You're welcome,' I say back.

'Now that that's done, are you ever going to tell me what happened with Luca?'

I look down at my hands then, like my skin has any visible marks of ever having had Luca with me, like I can somehow keep him here even though he's not.

Uncle Drew sighs. 'Look, kiddo. It's like I always say—fate is fixed, love is a thunderstorm, and Cheetos—'

'—are mankind's greatest invention since medicine and stuff. I know.' I grin at him, and he grins back.

'All I'm saying is, love isn't all that bad. Let Luca take care of your heart.'

And there it is. It's as simple as that, isn't it? There's nothing more terrifying yet rewarding at the same time—to relinquish control of both the now and the future to someone else, for someone else to affect how you smell the roses and taste the tea, to let them teach you how to fold napkins and chop veggies, to have someone take you on campus tours and fan meets, to allow someone else to build LEGO with you one brick at a time. To let someone in, to purposely *let* someone else take care of what you normally would yourself, to *let* someone else help you manage your heart.

And it's foolish and absurd and absolutely terrifying, but it's . . .

It's life. And the fear of death, the fear of things ending . . . it shouldn't stop me from going through my life anyway, because knowing that things won't last forever is what makes everything more beautiful.

'You know what?' I grin at my uncle. 'I don't think I'd like to talk about Luca right now. All I want to talk about is you.'

He grins back. 'What else is there to talk about? We talk here every day.'

'Yeah,' I say, 'I guess we do.'

He doesn't say anything else then, and the rays of the setting sun cast the whole corner booth in a finite glow. There is everything and nothing in the space between us now, and I'm suddenly overwhelmed by the million things I want to say. But all the questions and the regrets get stuck in my throat for some reason, and they all pale in comparison with the one, single thing that shines through the clutter in my heart, the most important thing I should've been telling my uncle day in and day out, both when he was alive and now that he's no longer here.

'I love you, Uncle Drew.'

It's all that I manage to whisper, but those five words are enough to summarize all the Cheetos and Netflix parties and the words I never got to say, those Discord memes and guild raids and that letter on my eighteenth birthday, the random surprises and Lumpy Space Princess and the little ponies on my desk. It's the only thing Uncle Drew needs to know, the only thing I want him to remember when he finally leaves.

A single tear trickles down my uncle's cheek. 'I love you too, Kali.'

At that moment, the CLOSED sign hanging by the door rattles, and the sound makes me whip my head around. There's no one there, though, but the moment I turn my head back to my uncle at the booth, there's no one there too.

That's it.

There's no fanfare, no bells and whistles, no blinding white light that signals my uncle heading off into a different plane or moving on to where he needs to go. There's just a sudden and unwelcome absence, a quiet loss.

It's only the oppressive void in front of me now, an empty corner booth and an empty seat and an empty heart, no warmth or smile or newsboy cap around, no ghostly image or note left in a hurry or even a curt goodbye. The injustice of it all batters against my chest and my tears get the better of me, hot and angry and helpless all at the same time.

I always thought I'd been given a second chance, a golden opportunity to keep my uncle with me every waking hour of the day. To be with him and bond with him and keep him with me forever, to stay in this infinite space in time where none of us could ever move on. But there are still so many things I want to do, so many things I want to say. I still didn't get a proper goodbye, but maybe that's just how it's supposed to be.

Maybe I'm not meant to say goodbye to my uncle, because when you love someone this deeply, no amount of time or second chances can ever prepare you for when they go away.

In the silence of the shop, I smile through the sobs, through the grip in my chest, through the heartbreak.

Just like that, Uncle Drew is gone.

Maybe This Time, That's Okay

Google Drive: Fire_Drewid@gmail.com
Password: cheetosFORlife75!
OPEN ONLY IN CASE OF AN EMERGENCY!!!!!!!
Swear, Kali. Swear on your level 97 Holy Diwata.

After the first warm dinner I had with my parents in a while,
I use Uncle Drew's login details to access his Google Drive.
Most of them are folders for every game review, every press
con, every media access event he's had with game devs over
the years. There are APKs for installing Android games and
emulators and free *Mitolohiya Mobile* in-game goodies. There
are assets for games and press kits and access codes. There
are unfinished drafts and published works and photos from
random demos.

But, amid all the clutter and the proofs of Uncle Drew's
life, there's a single folder that outshines the rest, and it
wrenches my attention from everything else.

It's a folder named 'Kali'.

With a deep breath and with the heat already pooling
against my eyelids, I click it open.

Inside are drafts of letters he never got to send, random
messages he planned to give me on my birthdays. The

memos to make special days more memorable, photos he took to piece together an unfinished collage, even voice clips of outtakes he wanted to surprise me with. Uncle Drew has planned out a schedule of messages for every birthday, and I click on one to hear him blurt out, 'Surprise! You've been surprised. Are you surprised?'

The joy in Uncle Drew's voice echoes throughout the emptiness of my room that night, sneaking into every nook and corner, weaving its way into the curtains and under the sheets. My fingers tremble. I click on a shaky video clip of him trying to record himself on his phone for my birthday next year, struggling with the sound quality as he attempted to be heard over the passing of the trains.

He beams at the camera with his newsboy cap and his never-fading grin and blurts out enthusiastic words of celebration that I can't make out with the way my tears have already clouded my vision. The idea of this message from the future mars me with the weight of the past, and finally, finally, Uncle Drew's absence sinks in.

There will be no more birthday wishes now, no silly surprises and plastic ponies on my desk. I won't see the ghost of his smile by the corner coffee shop and, maybe this time, that's okay.

I'm going to be okay.

I set Uncle Drew's video message to loop on my desktop media player, smiling through the haze in my eyes and the clearing cloud in my mind. Then, I close my eyes and let the tears fall, as Uncle Drew's voice serenades me through the night one last time.

* * *

When Mom drops me off across Tea for Two the next day, it's already begun. Mr Valencia contacted her about my attempts to save the shop, but he told her that after giving it much thought, he still decided to go with the client and tear it down anyway.

'I'm sorry, sweetie.' Mom tilted her head at me that morning, a new kind of head tilt I hadn't gotten from her before. It's not like everything is magically okay between us now, and it's not like she and Gua-ma actually believed me when I told them all about seeing Uncle Drew's ghost. But that afternoon was a key of sorts, something that unlocked our shared grief and opened communication channels between the three of us. We knew we were trapped inside Death's abyss, but we could rely on each other to share it and go through the dark together.

Which is why today, of all days, Mom decided to personally drop me off to witness the beginning of the end first-hand because it's the least she can do for me.

I trudge to the edge of the street, as far as the barriers let me, and my two best friends who got there earlier take their places on either side of me. They each take my hand in theirs, and the three of us gaze at the building, at all the machinery and the equipment and the debris and the goodbye.

What makes the whole thing worse is that Tea for Two isn't taken down instantaneously. It's not just a matter of a wrecking ball or an Acme Corporation dynamite stick. With the way the men in overalls are detaching windows, moving out the furniture, and salvaging the foundations piece by piece, it just feels like the universe is prolonging my agony as best as it can.

It seems silly now, how I spent all those afternoons hanging out with a ghost in the corner of what's now just an empty space. To punctuate this morbid display in front of me, two men take down the Tea for Two sign from the wall and the debris rains onto the ground. When the dust clears, I swear I almost make out a newsboy cap and a wayward smile, but the light shifts in the high heat of midday and it's gone.

Uncle Drew is gone.

Freyja squeezes my hand just as a rogue tear makes its way down my cheek. Ryan wraps an arm around me, and it's all I can do not to dash across the street and scour through the debris in a mad attempt to bring back an uncle that may or may not have been there. Tea for Two is nameless now, and just as the signage lies in shambles before us, my hopes of ever seeing my uncle again lay buried under the ruins too.

'So,' Freyja breaks the silence with her own version of the head tilt. 'What are we having for lunch?'

'Pizza or no lunch at all,' Ryan pipes in, and the two of them try to pry a smile out of me. I rub my nose with the back of my hand.

'Pizza it is,' I croak through the heaviness in my throat. 'But I'm not paying.'

'Of course not,' Ryan glances over at Frey with a knowing smile. 'The other future Atenean here is footing the bill.'

It takes a while for Ry's words to sink in, and when they do, I turn to Freyja with my eyes wide. 'You got in?'

Freyja's face flushes, the kind of flush that tells me that things are only going to get better from here. 'You were right. I talked to my parents about it, and they made arrangements. We can afford it, Kali. We just need to make certain sacrifices, but they told me a good education is a good education, and nothing is worth more than that.'

'Oh my god, Frey!' I swoop in for an embrace and she readily gives it to me. 'But what about your music?'

'They also told me not to give up on my passion—I know that now. So, I'll settle for music club for the meantime,' she breathes out over my shoulder. 'I'm going to effing take Ateneo by storm.'

'I'm so, so happy for you, Frey. For you both.' We break apart. 'Congratulations.'

'Save the congratulatory messages for graduation.' Ryan shakes his head. 'And speaking of celebrations . . . are we going to expect a certain barista boss to show up as someone's significant other that day?'

'Oh.' I scan across the street again. 'No. Luca's gone home to Cebu. He's . . . not coming back.'

'Why not?'

'Because I . . . sort of told him not to.'

Frey and Ry groan in unison, and a few people trying to cross the street at the intersection turn their heads at us.

'Kal, I don't want to sound insensitive, but isn't Uncle Drew the reason you didn't want to start anything with Luca in the first place?' Freyja clutches at her hair to exaggerate her frustration. 'What are you hanging around here for?'

'Frey's right, Kali. If you need any more convincing, let me ask you this,' Ryan grabs both my shoulders and stares into my eyes, 'did you ever stop to look—*really* look—at the petition you so desperately tried to pull together these past few weeks?'

'What do you mean?'

'I *mean*,' Ryan sighs, 'you've been too busy trying to collect all these signatures for your cause, but I don't think you ever read any of the comments people have been leaving on the petition page. You might have a personal goal with all this, but the people who offered you their signatures have their own cause too, and it's to save a treasured space that held so many memories for them.'

'It's not just about preserving what's there, Kali,' Frey pipes in. 'These people, these alumni, they want to keep the place as it is because of the memories they shared there, but that never stopped them from moving on with their lives, you know? They're out of high school, toughing it out in college or trying to survive their first jobs. They're parents now, business owners, professionals. They've had kids and are trying to navigate the tricky waters of parenthood. They've all grown up, Kali. They've all moved on.'

I look across the street again, at the corner where I last saw Uncle Drew, but then my gaze drifts a little to the right, at the space where the counter used to be, where Luca taught me about folding aprons and sampling college and brewing the perfect cup of tea. I stare at the space in front of the counter, the space where Frey sang the perfect song, the table where I forced Luca to sit still for half an hour, the aisle where customers lined up and that girl named Carlisle told me all about her mom's obsession with *Twilight*. I glance at the remnants of the back room, the wisps of Luca's engineering books and his faceless planners and the sticker nametags that had blanks for names on them.

'Old memories are lovely, Kali,' Ryan whispers beside me after a moment of silence. Then, he takes Freyja's hand, and they both smile at me. 'But new memories, the ones you're yet to make together . . . those are even more beautiful.'

I look at my two best friends now, at the naivete and the heartbreak and the happiness all rolled into one big wavering ball that's the future.

'I've said it before Ry, and I'll say it again: you're such a dweeb,' I grin at them both, and somehow, that weighted veil of grief around me doesn't seem so heavy. 'You both are, and I love you for it.'

Freyja rolls her eyes and the three of us hug each other right there in the middle of the sidewalk, gelled together by the uncertainty of the future and the possibility of more pizza over the horizon.

Before You Go

Graduation day sneaks up on me and it's all because of Mom. She and Dad sat me down to talk about college last night, and while I'm glad they no longer want to ship me off to Aunt Iris in Texas, it doesn't help that they want me to consider going to UST for a pre-med course.

Their wanting me to take up medicine is pretty cliche. Plus, I kinda want to go to Ateneo now. It's definitely because Frey and Ry will be there and definitely not because going to UST's campus again is just going to trigger all kinds of heartbreak for me.

But pre-med is better than getting shipped off miles and miles away, so I'll take what I can get. Although, to be honest, escaping oceans away to a different continent might just make the pain in my chest go away.

I never heard back from Luca. After that ridiculously eye-opening talk with my best friends on the sidewalk across Tea for Two, I asked Lee for that stupid blank planner back. I wanted to show Luca how much I had changed in a span of a few days, how wrong I was to push him away just because I was afraid of moving on in life. I filled it up with all kinds of plans for the future, intricate calendars of events that

I promised I'd do, even if it was just something as mundane as cleaning my room or adding some colour to my lifeless desk.

The planner being blank meant everything. Before long, I found myself pouring out all my hopes and dreams into it, scribbling plans like a madwoman and jotting down ideas of things I wanted to do and places I wanted to see. I spilled my dreams until I bled out, and, without even meaning to, I realized that I want Luca to be in every part of them.

The planner has become a confession of sorts. In it, I told Luca how Uncle Drew reconciled with his family and how he left, how it broke my heart and how things started getting easier with each passing day. I told him how I no longer keep seeing newsboy caps and Cheetos bags everywhere I go, no longer keep looking for excuses to revisit every old place. I still play *Mitolohiya Mobile* from time to time, but I no longer keep staring at Uncle Drew's forever-unchanging level. I no longer let my guilt keep me frozen in place, and when the day is over and the night creeps in, Death no longer keeps trying to get a hold of me.

I tell him how I spent one whole day cooped up in my room trying to piece together that mobile coffee cart, and now LEGO set number 40488 is complete. I slip a photo of it into the planner, the coffee cart sitting side-by-side with the boba tea shop we built together. Then, after I am all cried out from reminiscing about our memories and agonizing over all my regrets, I close the planner, scribble 'Before You Go' on the blank cover like Freyja's song predicted this whole damn mess and ask Lee to express mail it to him because I don't know his address and am not brave enough to ask.

It's been a week since I did that. I haven't received a single message from him.

'You sure you don't want in on this?' Freyja tucks her graduation cap under her armpit and shakes her hair loose after the ceremony. 'It's not every day you get to see Ryan shed his robot skin. Don't tell anyone.'

I giggle, and Ryan rolls his eyes beside Freyja. 'I'm sure. Besides, I think I want to go to Tea for Two for a bit. Just to walk around.'

They both look at each other with this weird glint in their eyes, and I sigh. 'And I *know* you're both going to tell me not to linger on the past and that it's all empty now and blah blah blah, but I just want to—'

'No, Kal.' Freyja gives me an odd smile that I can't quite place, and Ryan does the same. 'We . . . think it's a good idea. You should go.'

'Oh. Okay?' I raise an eyebrow at them, and they return my scepticism with an awkward wave before they turn around and join our batchmates. There's this after-grad party thing they're all headed off to and, for the first time, the ex-Queen Bee isn't interested.

Instead, I hop on a cab and head straight for Tea for Two—or what's left of it. I told Mom and Dad to go on ahead without me after the graduation ceremony was over, promising them I'd catch up with them over at Gua-ma's house. They were surprisingly agreeable, which is making me wonder if the universe is giving me a free pass for everything today.

Stepping off the cab onto the corner street, I immediately feel the shift in the air, the stillness of what was once Tea for Two, the absence of the life that used to buzz within its walls. It's been stripped down to its bare foundations now, just some steel frames here and there and a makeshift barrier that's been pieced together to keep the debris from spilling out onto the streets. Thankfully, given that it's a Sunday, there isn't any kind of work going on at the moment, offering me some momentary respite.

I step through the makeshift barriers and a wave of nostalgia welcomes me with an oppressive force. The debris crunches under my feet with every step until I reach the middle of the shop, and in the midst of the silence, I close my eyes and take a deep breath.

There's nothing here anymore, but that doesn't take away any of my memories. Those are real, and even though I'm moving on, I'll always carry them with me no matter how far into the future I go.

Thank you, Uncle Drew, I smile. *I miss you.*

'You're not supposed to be here.'

I literally jump at the sound of the voice behind me, and I almost trip on a wayward beam protruding from the rocky ground. 'Shit!'

'Shit is right.' A chuckle, then a laugh—familiar, heartbreaking.

I whip around in the direction of the voice I know too well. 'What are you doing here?'

'Shouldn't I be asking that question?' Luca throws me a lopsided grin, and I hate that even after all this time, it still has the same effect on me. Standing here in the middle of the ruins with the sunlight filtering through the cracks in the walls, he looks very much like a ghost himself in his white shirt and jeans and that stud in his ear. He has two hard hats in one hand and a small paper bag in the other. He reaches out to lay one of the hard hats on my head. 'I meant it when I said you shouldn't be here—you should be at your graduation, where I should be too.'

'I—' All the euphoria of seeing him again fries my brain to bits. 'What?'

'Your graduation.' He fastens the other hard hat on his head and looks down. 'I should've been there. Freyja gave me the exact time, but my flight was delayed.'

I frown. 'Again, *what?*'

He chuckles then. 'Ryan was texting me updates on the ceremony, but halfway through, I knew I wouldn't make it in time.'

I grit my teeth to tame the jumble of emotions in me. 'Ryan isn't the one you should be texting, is he?'

At this, Luca sighs and takes a step toward me. 'I'm sorry, Kali. I wanted it to be a surprise, and I even asked your parents to help me out to make sure I could get to you in time. But I didn't make it, and by the time I landed, your friends texted me you were coming here, so.'

'You—' I swallow. 'You asked my *parents?*'

'Um. Yeah.' Luca looks down again. 'Mr Valencia gave me their number.'

My jaw drops.

'I guess I should start from the beginning.' Luca peers up at me and bites his lip, effectively making this whole thing even harder for me. 'I started working on our cafe with my mom after I got back home, but not long after that, Mr Valencia called to tell me he's still pushing through with the demolition. I found it weird that he was calling me specifically just to update me about Tea for Two, but as it turns out, it wasn't the reason he called. He got in touch with me because he wanted to offer me a job.'

Luca shoves his free hand in his pocket, cool as ever despite the midday heat. 'He told me that what I said about the foundations made a lot of sense—he had the structure inspected himself, and he thought I had a lot of potential. So, he wanted me to work for him.' He shrugs. 'I told him I don't have a license, but he said he had a project manager I could shadow to gain some experience before retaking the exam.'

Fate is fixed, Uncle Drew had said. I guess he was right.

'It's ironic, isn't it? How Mr Valencia still somehow had a hand in this. Of course, I didn't accept the job right away because the whole point of flying home was to spend more time with my father. He thought it was a good opportunity for me, but I didn't want to leave as soon as I arrived, you know? But then your mail came, and I . . . I couldn't convince myself that it meant nothing. That *you* meant nothing.'

The summer crickets start a ruckus around us, but all it does is punctuate the emptiness of the shop. Luca takes another step closer. 'Dad said that anyone who goes through all that trouble just to reach me must see something in me, even if I can't see it myself. So I made a decision to come back. To you.

'I took your advice and reached out to my old friends too, but they're not the reason I'm here in Manila.' He shifts from one foot to another. 'Like I said, I wanted it to be a surprise—I guess it's one of those moments where I thought I could wow you with this huge thing from the movies you and Uncle Drew used to love so much. So, I enlisted Freyja and Ryan's help—after all, I wanted to make sure you didn't fall in love with anyone else while I was away.'

The corner of his lips tugs a little to the right. 'Then, I got in touch with your parents, and somehow managed to convince them not to ship you off miles and miles away from me. I sold them on the idea of UST, that it's a pretty good option too, but only if you want it to be. It's ultimately your choice, and they should be okay with that. And I also told them that I'd . . . I'd like to be with you, if they'll let me.'

A tinge of pink tints Luca's cheeks now, and he looks away for a second. 'That was honestly the most difficult thing I have ever done in my life, but I guess it all backfired when I couldn't even make it to your graduation in time.'

At this, he finally holds out the paper bag in his hand to me. 'So, I know I'm late, but . . . happy graduation.'

I've been in shock this whole time, honestly, so all I manage to do is take the bag from him and peer inside. There's a small LEGO box with roses on the cover. Set number 40460.

'I wanted to give you flowers but thought LEGO flowers would be better. And, uh, there are bigger options, to be honest, but I only had carry-on, so.' He smiles. 'We can build it together, if you want.'

After a few more seconds of staring at the box, I finally find my voice. 'Luca, I'm sorry.'

'Kali—'

'I'm sorry for pushing you away when all you ever did was take care of me. You helped me more than you can ever know, and I . . . I can't thank you enough for that.' My voice grows thick. 'You were right about Uncle Drew too—there was more than one way to save him, but in essence, you saved me too.'

He shakes his head. 'That's not possible.'

Luca takes one last step and closes the gap between us, and the feel of his lips on mine finally makes my tears fall. He wraps his arms around my waist and pulls me up even closer against him, and we stay locked that way until we both start to taste the salt from the tears trickling down my cheeks.

I feel him smile against my lips before we part, but he keeps my body against his like he's afraid to let go. 'Do me a favour,' he whispers in a low tone, 'and promise me you won't ever push me away again.'

I giggle despite my tears. 'I promise.'

He kisses my forehead and our hard hats clunk together with an awkward thunk. I giggle again, then lay my head on his shoulder.

He sighs. 'I'm sorry about Uncle Drew.'

'I'm sure he's enjoying unlimited Cheetos now, wherever he is. That reminds me.' I take one step away from Luca's embrace, and already it feels like a part of me is missing. 'I came here for a reason.'

'Which is?'

The rocks crumble underneath my Chucks as I make my way to where the corner booth used to be. Luca follows, just as I unhook the Cheetos pendant around my neck and lay it on the ground.

Uncle Drew always said that fate is fixed, love is a thunderstorm, and Cheetos are mankind's greatest invention since medicine and stuff.

I finally agree.

Luca wraps an arm around me just as I start to tremble again, but I take a deep breath and it somehow goes away.

The veil of grief is gone now, and maybe Death is finally setting me free.

Luca plants another kiss on my cheek. 'So, what now?'

'Now, you have to come with me to this graduation thing with my Gua-ma.' I turn to him with a smirk. 'Just because my parents apparently know you now doesn't mean you're off the hook. Gua-ma will grill you like a steak.'

'Well, shit.'

'Shit is right.'

Luca takes my hand in his. We step out of the rubble and into Lee's car, and as Luca starts up the engine, he offers me a moment to turn back to Tea for Two through the passenger seat window. My Cheetos pendant is all that's left of Uncle Drew in there now, and without me carrying it around my neck all the time, everything somehow feels lighter.

After a few more moments, Luca breathes out, 'Ready to go?'

'Yeah. I think I am.' I turn to him beside me. 'I know I am.'

He lays a hand over mine and squeezes. 'To your Gua-ma's?'

'Yes. This is the price you have to pay for Uncle Drew choosing you.'

He blinks at me. 'Choosing me?'

'Yeah.' I smile. 'He told me to let you take care of my heart.'

Luca doesn't say anything for a while, but his gaze tells me everything I need to know. It's a look filled with imperfect pasts and messy aprons and crowded supply runs, terrible train station coffee and planners filled to the brim with future plans. It's the look of LEGO sets just waiting to be built and memories waiting to be made, and maybe it's not the cleanest fold or the most perfect cup of tea or the best ramen in town, but it's him and me together, staying put and moving on at the same time.

'I think I'd be really, really good at that.'

'What?'

'Taking care of your heart.' He grins. 'You're not going to keep making me repeat myself, are you?'

And the memory of when we first met shines brighter now with a hopeful glow.

I smile back. 'No, sir.'

Epilogue

Kali unhooks the old Cheetos pendant around her neck. She lays the battered polymer clay figure on her open palm for a while, staring at the faded colours like she could see something else underneath the grime. For a second, it almost looks like she's about to put it back on, but then she holds her other palm onto the open one, pauses to take a deep breath, then bends down to set the Cheetos pendant on the rocky ground.

She takes a moment for herself before rising back up again. Luca wraps an arm around her when she starts to tremble, planting a kiss on her cheek like an unspoken promise. When he feels like she's ready, he takes her hand in his, and they step out of the coffee shop, hand-in-hand, hopeful, happy.

A middle-aged man watches this whole scene unfold before him from the distance, far enough to make it feel like it's a scene from a movie, but close enough that he can almost reach out and touch Kali himself. There's an odd sensation inside him, all around him. He's here but he's not here, and it's a perpetual disquiet, an unsettling little thing.

'Ready to go, Andrew?'

Andrew turns to the voice beside him, odd yet familiar, like he's only just met this stranger but he's also known him all his life. He adjusts the newsboy cap on his head and frowns. 'Uh, excuse me?'

'I simply asked if you were ready to go,' the voice beside him repeats. Andrew squints to clear his vision as, all of a sudden, everything around him feels blindingly bright. A few seconds of utter confusion later, the figure beside him materializes into something his eyes and his brain can recognize—the shape of a man his age, nameless and faceless, but warm and comforting at the same time.

'Um. No?' Andrew blinks again. 'Where are we going, exactly? And do I know you?'

'You could say that.' The figure shrugs, and Andrew can somehow tell that it's smiling despite the blurry edges. 'As for where we're going, I think you already know.'

'Do I?' Andrew turns back to the scene in front of him, and he sees Kali and Luca getting into a car and driving off to a future away from the shop, away from him. For the first time ever, he knows nothing about Kali's life. The Cheetos pendant has been left behind, and he doesn't know what's going to happen next.

'Are you sure about what you've done?' the figure asks. 'It couldn't have been easy.'

Somehow, Andrew knows exactly what the figure is talking about. He stares at the Cheetos pendant on the ground, somehow inside the ruins of Tea for Two now. Everything shifts around him then, moments going back in time, debris piecing itself back together, walls being rebuilt and the roof sealing itself back overhead. The furniture rewinds and it's him and his niece in the corner booth, the CLOSED sign on the door rattling, Kali turning her head, and him choosing to leave without another word.

He *chose* to leave.

And that, as it turns out, is the key to it after all.

'It broke your heart, didn't it?' the figure whispers, and Andrew feels a gentle breeze envelope him in an embrace.

'It did.' He sighs. 'But I had to do it.'

'Do what?'

Andrew lets the heartbreak wash over him one last time. 'I had to let her go.'

'Then you're ready,' the figure says again.

Andrew tears his eyes away from the scene in front of him. 'What do you mean?'

'That thing you've been searching for. Why you couldn't leave?' The figure smiles. 'You had to let her go, Andrew. That was all you had to do.'

'Oh.' Andrew looks down now, but when the tears come, it doesn't hurt. There's no squeezing pain in his chest, no choking feeling, no sensation of regret or loss or pain. It feels brighter, lighter. It feels . . . good. Like it's different.

Like he's finally found where he belongs.

'Turns out I'm ready, I guess.' Andrew smiles through the tears in his eyes. 'Let's go.'

The figure smiles again, and Andrew feels hope and joy and happiness radiate around him all at the same time.

Above all, he feels peace.

They both turn around and start walking. 'So,' the figure wraps an arm around his shoulders like it's welcoming an old friend.

'I hear you like Cheetos.'

Acknowledgements

The Summer of Letting Go is my first Penguin book that didn't take more than four years to write, but that doesn't mean it was the least bit easy. Writing about loss always leaves a hole in my heart. Each book I write takes a significant chunk out of it—broken off and woven into the pages of each story. I hope that, after my heart has bled onto the pages, you'll find a tale worth keeping in yours long after the last chapter ends.

Thank you, as always, to KB Meniado who's been instrumental to every single book I've ever written—you'll always be a ray of light, a beacon of hope, a forever-cheerleader, the best beta-reader–editor, and my Cebuano-phrase provider. I'm so glad our paths crossed—the #romanceclass and #BRUMultiverse bond is strong and unbreakable, and I'll forever be grateful to this community for championing what love should and can be. My eternal gratitude goes out to Bryce King, yet again, for lawyering up as always (Tea for Two milk tea on me) and to my BFF Stephanie Sia—I want you to know that the distance and the sadness may grow bigger, but the love will always stay the same, no matter where life takes us.

Thank you to Iris Siy for believing in me so much and so constantly—you will always be the better version of Kali's

Frey and Ryan for me—and to all of my closest friends, near or far, who support me in their own ways.

To my Scribe Tribe—Kayce Teo, Joyce Chua, Eva Wong Nava, and Marga Ortigas—I can't thank my lucky stars enough that you deemed me worthy to be in this shared space together, and I will always be honoured to have you not just as my fellow wordsmiths but also as my friends and forever endorsers!

To my kick-ass street team and all of the bibliophiles I've bonded with on Instagram—thank you for generously giving your time and love to gush about my odd little stories. I've had so many ups and downs throughout this often-lonely author journey but having you all here and knowing I'm not alone means more to me than you can ever imagine. Thank you for readers like you who give life to these kinds of tales, for talking about them and in some way encouraging more of these stories so that writers can write more of them and unleash them into the world.

My heartfelt appreciation goes out to the tight-knit Penguin Random House SEA family—we are all in this together, and I will always feel privileged to be on this rollercoaster ride with you all. To Melvin Choo and Dots Ngo, thank you for tirelessly toiling behind the scenes to push our books out—the world is a difficult place but having you by our side makes the fight worthwhile.

Of course, none of this would be possible without the PRH SEA angels, with a special shoutout to Thatchaa who labours over my stories like they're her own book babies too; Sneha who sharpened and polished this story to be in the best shape it can possibly be while leaving heartwarming encouragements in between the lines; the dynamic duo of

Garima and Chai whose ideas are always on fire and whose love, support, and unparalleled hard work are proof of how every book is not just a job for them but also a part of them personally; Almira who waves her magic behind the distribution lines and makes me suspect she's an actual wizard; and, as always, Nora, who gets so many emails and messages from me but never fails to cheer me on, never fails to support my endeavours from the sidelines in silence, and who even told me she couldn't wait to see how hot Luca was when I first pitched the idea to her. Thank you, Nora, for believing in my stories, always.

Obviously, my very first fans back when I haphazardly stapled together my handwritten 'books' when I was eight will always be my parents and my brother—thank you for tolerating my oddities. To my husband, thank you for spending excruciatingly long hours with me, thinking of ways to solve problems with my narratives or trying to come up with bigger, better, grander ideas with every burst of inspiration. And, most important of all, thank you to the Big Guy up there, who started it all in the first place, without whom, I wouldn't be here.

Last but not least, thank you, dear reader, for going through Kali's journey of moving on and letting go. I started the story harmlessly enough, but it started shaping up into a tearjerker as I was writing it because of all the words I desperately wanted to say—and, like Kali said, 'Maybe this time, that's okay.' I hope that the raw emotions resonated with you in some way, whether they be giddy young-love feels or good cathartic tears.

So, 'before you go, before you go', let's have some tea at Tea for Two or share a bag of Cheetos?

Book Club Questions

1. The themes of loss and grief are very much front and centre in this book. How do you think this is portrayed through the physical representation of a ghost?
2. Which character did you relate to the most and why?
3. What do the LEGO bricks symbolize in the context of Kali's personality? And Luca's?
4. What do the blank planners symbolize in the context of Kali's personality? And Luca's?
5. What do you think happens to Kali and Luca after the book's official ending? And to Uncle Drew?
6. What is the significance of the title? Did you find it meaningful? Why or why not?
7. How has Kali's family upbringing affected her personality? How about Luca's upbringing?
8. Were there times you disagreed with Kali's actions? What would you have done differently?
9. Looking at the story from Luca's perspective, do you agree or disagree with his actions?
10. How do the first scene and the last scene tie together?
11. What scene resonated with you the most at a personal level?

12. How did you feel about the ending?
13. In the end, what do you think it really means to save Uncle Drew?
14. List down the most quotable quotes in your opinion.
15. If you could come up with your own mantra, what would you add to, 'Fate is fixed, love is a thunderstorm, and ___ ?'